ABOUT THIS BOOK

Infiniti Clausman is making the most of senior year. Throwing parties, pulling pranks, and breaking all the rules, she's determined to graduate with a bang! But there's one thing on her senior year bucket list she hasn't been able to cross off yet—falling in love. In fact, she's never even been kissed.

Infiniti hopes to change this when she travels from Houston to Colorado for the holiday break. Instead, she finds her world turned upside down when she discovers all things supernatural exist, time travel is real, and her very life is at stake. Suddenly, that kiss is the least of her worries.

Joe Greg will never forget the injured girl he and Kase Kasun found on the side of the mountain. It was 2012, and he was only twelve, but the image of the wreckage and his interaction with the girl has never left him. When he sees the girl again in 2018, she looks exactly the same. He figures out that she's time-traveled to his present, with a reaper on her heels and a mystery to unravel. Drawn to protect her, he's hell-bent on standing by her side. Even if it means his death.

HAVENWOOD FALLS HIGH BOOKS

Written in the Stars by Kallie Ross

Reawakened by Morgan Wylie

The Fall by Kristen Yard

Somewhere Within by Amy Hale

Awaken the Soul by Michele G. Miller

Bound by Shadows by Cameo Renae

Fata Morgana by E.J. Fechenda

Forever Emeline by Katie M. John

Reclamation by AnnaLisa Grant

Avenoir by Daniele Lanzarotta

Avenge the Heart by Michele G. Miller

Curse the Night by R.K. Ryals

Blood & Iron by Amy Hale

Shadows & Spells by Cameo Renae

Falling Deep by J.L. Weil

Saving Infiniti by Rose Garcia

Willful by Liz Ferry

Cast in Moonlight by Ali Winters

Promise the Moon by Kallie Ross

Blurred Lines by Daniele Lanzarotta

Ascending Darkness by J.L. Weil

Finding Infiniti by Rose Garcia

Unicorn's Lament by Megan Linski

Paper Bird by Amy Richie

Predestined by Valia Lind

Rediscovered by Morgan Wylie

Ashes of Fate by Apryl Baker

Stay up to date at www.HavenwoodFalls.com

ALSO BY ROSE GARCIA

Final Life

Final Stand

Final Death

First Life

SAVING INFINITI

A HAVENWOOD FALLS HIGH NOVELLA

ROSE GARCIA

To everyone who believes in one true love.

CHAPTER 1

$\mathcal{F}$leet ran his fingers through his dark hair before tilting his head toward the night sky. He eyed the top floor of the Houston skyscraper Tavion had called home since tracking Dominique and her protectors to the oversized Texas city. A cool December breeze swept through the streets, kicking up the stench of trash from a nearby dumpster. Fleet hated all the concrete, all the glass buildings, but mostly he hated taking on the role of being one of the Tainted and on Tavion's side against the Pures. He had accepted the directive for the greater good, but the passing of so many years had started to muddle allegiances in his brain. All sense of right and wrong had started to merge. Too good at his job, he found himself alone and sure of nothing but the perpetual clench in his gut.

Fleet closed his eyes. He tried not to picture the horrible things he had done in Tavion's name while tracking Dominique, but had a hard time suppressing the images. His only solace was knowing that in this life, her final life, Dominique had no recollection of any of her prior lives. Even if it meant forgetting him forever, Fleet hoped Dominique's memories would never return. There was too much pain and suffering for anyone to have to recall, let alone someone he secretly cared about.

Fleet banged his fist against the glass wall of the downtown apartment building. "Get your shit together, man."

Pressing his palm against the cool surface, he held his breath, then let it trickle out between clenched teeth. He had built a brick wall around his true feelings for Dominique and the Pures ages ago, vowing not to let anyone ever see that side of himself, especially Tavion. He had a job to do and was determined to see it through no matter what. To hell with what anyone thought of him.

"Don't let anyone in," he muttered, while strengthening the fortress of his mind. With his vulnerabilities hidden, he turned his focus to Tavion's directive: find Dominique and prepare her for death.

"I got this," he whispered to himself. "I can do this."

With his emotions in check, he jerked the heavy door open. He nodded at the security guard behind the holiday-adorned lobby desk. The guard peered at him from over his computer screen.

"Hey, Fleet. Your boss is in quite a mood tonight." He whistled. "Quite a mood."

Fleet knew exactly what sort of mood Tavion was in. Starving for death and destruction, he displayed hatred like a neon sign. But some days his harsh light shone brighter than usual. Today must have been one of those days.

"Thanks, Sammy."

Sammy said something else about Christmas spirit and holiday joy, but Fleet ignored him. Joy didn't exist for him, hadn't in a long time. And it wasn't likely to ever return.

Pushing the button for the top floor with his key card, Fleet repeated his mission over and over in his mind, drowning out the doubt that lingered in the darkest corners. With a ding, the steel doors opened. He loathed interacting with Tavion and mostly operated on his own, but every now and again Tavion would call him in for a status report.

Fleet steadied himself. He cleared his mind. He stepped into the all-white foyer of the sprawling penthouse. Thick silence and heavy foreboding sucked the air right out of the space. He knew this meeting, like all the others, was going to suck.

Windows lined the long L-shaped living space that looked out on the sparkling buildings of the massive city. The dark sky outside blended in with the shadowy room. Only the soft light from the gleaming neighboring structures gave any indication of life in the space. An oversized brown leather chair facing the view was the lone piece of furniture in the entire apartment. It was Tavion's favorite spot.

Tavion extended his arm over the armrest. He waved Fleet over.

"Come."

Fleet's boots thudded against the marble floors, the echo of each step bouncing all around him like a lonely symphony. He took his place next to Tavion and clasped his hands behind his leather jacket. Glancing at Tavion, he saw that he was dressed in his usual black suit. His profile revealed a deep scowl.

"How may I help you, sir?"

Tavion moved his long skeletal fingers to his pale face and started rubbing his chin. "Dominique Wells," he said, letting the *s* trickle out of his mouth as if he were a slithering snake. "I've been thinking of her final life, and the differences here as compared to our other lives, and I do not like it. The events of late do not sit well with me. This year in particular, 2012, is fraught with too many unknowns."

Fleet remembered a time when Tavion's appearance was hardy and robust. Tavion had once stood on the side of right, but over time, a deep-seated hatred toward mankind pulled him away. Tavion detested humans and blamed them for the gradual destruction of the natural world. His departure split the Transhumans into two factions: the good became known as the Pure. The evil became known as the Tainted, and Tavion became their leader. He eventually marked Dominique for death in an attempt to get back at the Pure. With each passing decade, Tavion's hate grew in his heart and in his body, reducing him to his current death-like appearance.

Yet Fleet knew Tavion was right. Things in this life were way different, mainly with the involvement of first lifers Trent Avila and Infiniti Clausman. Friends of Dominique's, Fleet suspected they'd play a role in Dominique's quest for survival. It seemed Tavion shared the same sentiment.

Testing his theory, Fleet asked, "What do you mean?"

Tavion let out a low growl. "Do not pretend that you know not of what I speak." He stood and faced Fleet. "Or are you keeping something from me?"

Hiding his surprise at the threatening move, Fleet eyed Tavion with matching menace, a look he knew Tavion respected. Tavion resided in perpetual paranoia, forcing Fleet to work overtime to keep Tavion's trust secured.

Fleet raised his chin. "I assure you, I am not keeping anything from you, sir. Nor would I make pretense."

Fleet waited for Tavion's response, wondering if Tavion had somehow discovered the conflict within him. Fleet curled his fingers behind his back, ready to form an energy ball and strike Tavion if needed. Luckily, Tavion's face softened. He placed his hand on Fleet's shoulder.

"My apologies, Fleet. I should not be so angry with you, especially since you are the only one I've been able to count on all these very long years."

Fleet relaxed his fist, but his body remained tense. "It's okay, sir."

Tavion eased back down on his chair. He returned his gaze to the twinkling lights of the downtown buildings. "Dominique keeps eluding us, but I know she's close. I can feel her fear, can practically smell her blood. Her parents cannot hide her forever. Eventually there'll be another break, and we'll find her. In the meantime, I want you to follow this one."

Tavion let loose a dark mist from his palm. It gathered into a swirl, forming a large oval shape. The mist thinned out, revealing an image of Infiniti Clausman, Dominique's neighbor and friend. Petite with small features and long dark hair, she danced around her room while packing a suitcase.

"This first lifer is important," Tavion said. "I can sense it."

Just as Fleet suspected, she *was* important. He thought of the other first lifer.

"What of Trent Avila?"

"Leave him to me." Tavion jabbed his finger at the floating image. "But this one is leaving in the morning with her mother on a holiday trip, and I want you on her heels. You will follow her to Colorado. I want to know everything about her. Understood? What she eats, what she drinks, what she loves, what she fears. All of it."

By the look of her room and the way she carried herself, she seemed like an average teenager of the time—interested in parties, music, and all things superficial. Yet something about her had struck a chord with Tavion. Fleet, too. There had to be more to her, but what?

"Understood, sir."

Tavion whisked the image away. He dismissed Fleet with a wave. "Go."

A sinking feeling grew in the pit of Fleet's stomach as he rode the elevator down to the first floor. He'd never been away from Dominique before. He didn't want to risk Tavion finding her while he was gone, yet he also didn't want Tavion to know about the conflict within him. Should he abandon Tavion's directive? Or should he follow Infiniti to Colorado and trust that Dominique would not be found until he returned?

Back outside, Fleet paced up and down the sidewalk, his mind on overdrive. Everything had repeated perfectly from lifetime to lifetime, but in this life nothing was the same. Nothing! And it was driving him crazy.

"It's better that way," a small voice said.

Fleet whipped around and saw a young girl. No more than five years old, she wore a long white dress that matched her long hair. She studied him with oversized green eyes.

"What's better?" he asked.

"That everything is different in this life."

A million things raced through Fleet's mind. Before he could say anything, the girl went on.

"You need to follow her. She will need you."

"The first lifer?"

"Yes. Infiniti. She will need you in Colorado."

A pink shimmery hue radiated from her body. Recognizing the young girl as part of the spirit world, yet sensing something familiar about her, he peered at her with questioning eyes. He moved closer.

"Who are you?"

The girl lifted her skirt off the floor with dainty hands and gave an old-fashioned curtsey. "I am Abigail. It's nice to meet you." Her innocent face flashed with remorse. "I used to be like you, but then I died. I had to in order to help save Dominique. Her friend is my friend, and Infiniti is important. Everyone in this life is. So you see, that's why you need to follow her. You need to help her."

Fleet latched on to her statement about being like him, but had no idea what she meant. Before he could ask her to explain, she stepped forward. She held out her hand, as if she wanted to touch him, but then dropped her arm. She lowered her head, her shoulders sagged, and she looked as if she might burst into tears.

"I am so sorry about what you are going through. I really am."

He looked about to see if anyone was around to witness the conversation he was having with the spirit girl, but the streets were empty. When he turned back to Abigail, she was gone.

"Hey! Come back!"

Desperate to ask the girl more questions, he waited a few minutes for her to return, but she didn't. He clasped his hands behind his neck. He walked up and down the sidewalk. He had no idea what she meant about feeling sorry for him, but figured it had to do with him joining Tavion's ranks. Shit, even he felt sorry for himself. He eyed the night sky that had begun to lighten to a soft gray. If Infiniti was important enough to garner Tavion's attention, then she probably would need his help.

"Guess I'm going to Colorado."

6

CHAPTER 2

*I*nfiniti clutched the armrests of her seat as the plane from Houston to Denver bobbed up and down. Glancing next to her, she saw her mom's usual scotch and soda splash over the edge of the plastic cup as she struggled with puckered lips to get the liquid into her mouth. Infiniti wished she had a drink of her own.

"Maybe I'm being punished," Infiniti said to her mother, her anxiety on overload. Streaks of light shot through dark clouds. Rain pelted her window. Rumbling thunder shook the plane. "Maybe we should've left on Friday instead of today. Maybe I should've stayed for that dumb test."

"Fin, no one is being punished. Okay? Your teacher said the test was optional. Leaving on a Wednesday will give us more time with the cousins." Infiniti's mom sipped her drink. "Relax."

Infiniti's gut twinged because her teacher hadn't exactly said that. Pushing aside her guilt, she fished through her backpack, searching for her pack of gum. Finding the cinnamon sticks, she unwrapped them and shoved three into her mouth. Terrified of crashing, Infiniti's mind raced with all things she hadn't done yet with her life—graduate, get a tattoo, go to college, backpack across Europe, fall in love. She hadn't even had her first kiss yet. Her stomach twisted tight with fear and regret.

"We can't die. We just can't."

"We're not dying, Fin," her mom admonished between each hard-earned sip. "It's going to be fine. It's only turbulence."

With a sharp drop, the drink tumbled out of her mother's grasp. Luggage careened from the overhead bins. Oxygen masks released overhead. Infiniti wanted to yell, but her voice was strangled in her throat.

Infiniti's mom flew into action mode. She grasped Infiniti's arm with one hand, hollered commands Infiniti couldn't hear over the shouting all around them, and yanked at the masks. She slipped hers on with frantic motions.

Infiniti knew she should be doing the same, but couldn't move a muscle toward the life-saving plastic bag. Her mother swooped in. She snatched at the mask in front of Infiniti. She wrestled with the cords, like a woman possessed.

Images of death and wreckage blasted through Infiniti's mind. This was it. Game over! She burned with the sudden need to confess all the crap she'd done, because there was no way they were going to survive this.

She stopped her mom from slamming the mask on her face. "Mom, I'm sorry about all the sneaking out, smoking weed, skipping school, and throwing parties every time you went out of town! I'm sorry for all of it! And I lied about the test being optional!"

The plane leveled out. The blinking emergency lights turned off. Infiniti's mom tore off her mask.

"Really?" Her mom narrowed her eyes. She sat back in her chair, both masks dangling before them now. "Dammit, Infiniti Marie."

Infiniti gulped. She spotted the wad of gum on her pant leg, wondering when it had dropped out of her mouth. She scooped it up and slipped it between her lips.

"Mom, we were—"

Her mom cut her off with a raised finger. "That's your one get-out-of-jail-free card. Got it, young lady?"

"Yeah, got it. But—"

"Infiniti, stop. Not another word."

Feeling like a crappy daughter, and debating whether she should beg for forgiveness despite her mom telling her to be quiet, the pilot saved her with an announcement.

"Ladies and gentlemen, apologies for the rough ride. The skies have not been very friendly today, and I've received word that the Denver area is taking a beating right now. We'll be landing at Montrose Regional Airport instead. Personnel will be at the gate once you deplane to assist with connecting flights and answer any questions you may have. My apologies once again, folks. Flight attendants, prepare for landing."

After a bumpy landing, Infiniti and her mom managed to find a room at a small inn not far from the airport. They were even lucky enough to secure a rental car in case the airport became backlogged due to all the rerouted and canceled flights. Snuggled in their beds for the night and grateful to be alive, Infiniti whispered to her mom.

"Mom, I'm really sorry."

"I know, honey. I am, too. But we're alive, and all is good. Now let's get some sleep."

Infiniti tossed and turned while visions of fiery crashes cluttered her mind. She rearranged her pillow at least a hundred times, hoping to find the perfect level of fluffiness for her head. She shifted her legs from tucked up to her chest to splayed out. It took forever for her to fall asleep, and when she finally did, she was jarred awake by her phone alarm. She grumbled at herself for not remembering to turn it off, but it was too late. She was awake again. She brought her phone close to her face and saw that it was eight in the morning. How long had she actually slept?

Not exactly wanting to be awake yet, and finding it hard to breathe because of the high altitude, she decided to go ahead and get out of bed. With a groan, she trudged her weary bones to the window and opened the curtains of their small first floor room. She couldn't believe her eyes. Snow was piled all the way to the top of the glass. It was as if their room was nestled inside a giant sno-cone. A wave of cold air seeped into the room with the fabric pulled back, even though the heater was cranked.

"This is crazy. Mom, come over here." Infiniti held her hand up to the window. "I'm not even touching the glass, and my hand is freezing."

Infiniti's mom rubbed her eyes. "Really?" she asked with a yawn. She put on her glasses and joined Infiniti. They stood together eyeing the white snow. "Oh, no. Looks like we may not make it to Breck this holiday." Sensing Infiniti's disappointment, since missing out on Breckenridge meant not seeing their cousins who were already there, Infiniti's mom tacked on, "But who knows? Maybe it'll clear out soon."

Infiniti perked up. "Yeah!" Then her stomach growled. "But whatever we do, we need food."

"Yes, we do," her mom said, rubbing her forehead. "And electrolytes. My head is killing me, and I'm having a hard time breathing."

"I'm feeling it, too," Infiniti said as her mom set up her laptop on a small desk in the corner of the room. "Why don't you stay here and search for flight information while I find us some drinks and food."

"Good idea," her mom agreed.

Infiniti quickly got dressed. She studied herself in the mirror. Dark jeans, a red sweater, her favorite black boots with fur at the top. She thought her outfit looked pretty cute. She ran her fingers through her hair, trying to revive the curls that had flattened without the humidity. They refused to bounce back to life, but she didn't mind. She liked how long her hair was when it was straight.

She dotted some concealer on the dark circles under her eyes, then puckered her lips and put on some gloss. She wanted to look decent in case she ran into any hot guys while exploring the inn. Boy crazy for as long as she could remember, keeping an eye out for hotties was her favorite hobby, especially when she was out of town. Plus, she had her senior year bucket list to keep in mind, with the number one item being to fall in love. Or deep like. Or anything close. Really, she just wanted a kiss.

She wrapped her wallet strap around her wrist. "Be right back!"

Stepping into the hallway, she caught a glimpse of someone

coming her way. She backed up to her door so she wouldn't run into anyone, but when she faced the direction of the passerby, nobody was there. Her spine tingled. Her stomach dropped.

"What the?" she asked herself in a whisper, swearing she had seen someone in her peripheral vision.

Examining the red-carpeted hallway and the dark wood walls, a crazy notion dawned on her. Maybe the inn was haunted. Shivers raced across her arms. The decor certainly matched the spooky vibe. She loved all things supernatural but had never come face to face with a ghost or anything. She had a Ouija board at home, a new deck of oracle cards from her spiritual neighbor Jan, and a penchant for watching scary movies, but nothing otherworldly had ever happened to her.

Panic mixed with excitement stirred in her. She stepped away from the door and into the middle of the hallway.

"Um, hello? Anybody there?"

She waved her hands out in front her, as if she could touch a ghost if one had been near. With no response, she shook her head, dismissing the idea of paranormal activity. She looked around to make sure no one had witnessed her waving her arms in the hallway like a crazy person. She blew out a heavy breath, relieved to not see anyone. A fresh rumble in her stomach reminded her of her food-gathering task.

"Come on," she muttered to herself.

She made her way down the hall with a brisk stride. Turning the corner, she emerged into a quaint woodsy lobby. With their late arrival the night before and chaos from the small crowd checking in from the airport, Infiniti hadn't had the time to scope out the place. With the dawn of the new day, she was able to take it all in.

The inn could've served as a location for a sweet and cheesy holiday movie. A roaring fire crackled in a massive stone fireplace in the middle of the room with gorgeous hand-knit stockings hanging from the chunky wooden mantle. An assortment of animal hides adorned the dark wood floors. Antlers and pictures of scenic landscapes hung on the wood-paneled walls. A short and stout

Christmas tree stood by the front door. Infiniti couldn't help but feel merry and hopeful. But what made everything even better was the scent of cinnamon coffee that wafted her way. Her mouth watered.

Scanning the area for the source of the goodness, she spotted a small café on the other side of the twinkling tree. A handful of people hovered near the counter. Taking her spot in line, she overheard their conversations. Most were chatting about the big snow storm, how they had other destinations to make, and how they'd been hounding the airlines for updates. When it was her turn to order, she was lucky enough to get coffee for her and her mom, and two small croissants. All the other breakfast items were sold out.

"The roads have all been plowed in the area if you want to venture out for food," the nice grandma looking lady behind the counter suggested.

Sipping the warm liquid, Infiniti thanked her for the tip. With her coffee and food in hand, she went back to her room.

"I've got coffee and two small croissants. But the lady at the café said the roads were clear and suggested I go out for food. Is that cool with you?"

Her mom had buried herself in something work-related on her laptop. She took a few seconds to answer. "Yeah, yeah, that's fine. I've got this matter to handle real quick anyway."

"Okay," Infiniti answered. "Text me if you need me."

Wearing her new puffy black coat, she hurried out of the inn and to the parking lot. Expecting the car to be piled high in snow, she found it had been scraped and cleaned off.

"That was cool," she said, thinking someone from the inn had done it, because all the cars looked the same.

Infiniti cranked the heater in the beige four-door rental. Waiting for the car to warm, she scanned the radio stations for music. Finally finding some decent tunes, she rolled out of the inn parking lot and headed down the street.

Mounds of snow lined both sides of the small road, but that didn't intimidate her. She'd spent several holidays driving around Breckenridge in the snow and sleet; she could definitely handle a freshly plowed road. Eyeing the gray skies, she took the lack of falling snow as a good sign.

"Yep, everything's gonna be all right, all right, all right."

Passing by cute cottages, most of which were decked out with Christmas wreaths and other holiday decor, Infiniti finally came upon an intersection. A small grocery sat on the corner, nestled behind a row of magnificent blue spruce trees. With her stomach on hunger overdrive, she parked and dashed inside the store. She maneuvered up and down the aisles with speed. Finished with her shopping spree, she eyed her cart, thinking she probably had too much stuff, but didn't care. She was starving, and she was pretty sure her mom was, too. The food would not be wasted.

Back in her car, she fished through the grocery sacks. She pulled out a sports drink that promised a high percentage of electrolytes and a bag of Flamin' Hot Cheetos. With one hand on the wheel and the other on her favorite snack, she moved the bag to her mouth and ripped open the top with her teeth. A cluster of Cheetos poured into her mouth.

"Oh my God, yes," she moaned with each crunchy bite. Setting the bag down, she chugged her drink.

Feeling a ton better with food and drink in her stomach, she decided to take a quick, self-guided tour of the town. Since her mom hadn't called or texted yet, she figured she had some time to spare. She loved new places, and the mountain town was too cute to not explore. Passing rows and rows of the most adorable homes, she eventually found herself on a two-lane road. She admired the majestic mountains, the snow-blanketed terrain, and the enormous trees that hung on to clumps of white.

Driving around and digging into a second bag of Cheetos, Infiniti was totally caught up in the sights when she noticed a shadowy movement from the corner of her eye. Her stomach dropped, her hands shook, and her Cheetos bag fell from her hands. She wondered if a ghost had followed her from the inn.

She lifted her foot off the accelerator and coasted for a bit. She held her breath. She eyed the space to the right. She looked at the backseat through her rearview mirror. Not seeing anything, she let the air trickle out of her mouth. A nervous laugh escaped her lips.

"Stupid altitude. Now I'm hallucinating."

She started to speed up again when a hard shudder passed through her body. Every light inside the car started flickering. Blaring static took over the music. She slammed on the brakes, screeched to a stop, and hopped out of the car.

"What the hell!"

Her heart slammed against her chest. Her body shivered, and not just from the winter cold. She peered into the car through the open door.

"If there's a ghost in there, go away!" She thought of some of her favorite horror movies, trying to recall the correct words to use against an evil spirit. She made a cross sign with her fingers. "The power of Christ compels you!"

She dropped her hands, thinking she probably sounded crazy because she knew she did. She looked up and down the road, hoping someone would drive by and help her, but the roads were empty. But then she wondered what she'd even say to someone passing by. "Uh, excuse me, there may be a ghost in my car. Can you help?" Yeah, that would go over well. She mustered up her courage and moved closer to the rental, ready to take on her ghost by herself.

"I'm getting in the car now and driving back to the inn," she declared. "And you'd better leave me alone!" She added for good measure, "You are not welcome here!"

Easing herself back onto her seat, her hands shaking like crazy, she turned the car around so she could haul ass back the way she had come. Suddenly, she became aware that her mom hadn't called her. In fact, her phone hadn't made a sound in a long while. How much time had passed anyway?

She picked up her phone from the cup holder and brought it to her face. No service.

"Uh oh," she muttered, wondering how long her phone had been like that, knowing full well that her mom was probably going out of her mind. "She's gonna be so pissed."

She accelerated to a high speed while trying to call her mom over and over with frantic fingers, hoping she'd hit a pocket of cell service. She lifted her phone up in the air while at the same time pressing the redial button, but her phone tumbled from her grasp and onto the seat next to her. She let out an exasperated grunt. She stretched her fingers for it, but the phone was out of reach. She scooted over and made a lunging grab. Her fingertips barely made contact with the device. She scooted the phone closer with a flick and scooped it up.

"Yes!" she proclaimed.

With her phone in hand, she brought her eyes back to the road and saw that she had veered into the wrong lane.

"Shit!"

She jerked her wheel to get her car back over, sending the car into a fishtail. The sedan spun out of control. She took her foot off the pedal, her hands off the wheel, and started screaming.

Flashes of snow and trees whirred before her. Her mind raced with crazy thoughts of how she had survived a near plane crash only to die here on this stupid mountain. Alone. Never having been freakin' kissed. Also, her mom would never forgive her!

Her body lifted off the seat. Her seatbelt engaged, holding her down with a tug. A lone red Cheeto sailed across her line of sight. Her hair flew about her face. And that's when she realized the entire freaking car had plunged off the side of the road.

She sucked in her breath. She closed her eyes. She squeaked out an "eep" as a roar sounded in her ears.

CHAPTER 3

$\mathcal{F}$ ocusing on his energy, Fleet let loose a stream of gray mist from his hands. The warm haze seeped over every inch of him, turning translucent and covering his body like a second skin. The mist rendered him invisible and would stay there until he willed it away.

Staying close, he followed Infiniti and her mom. From the backseat of their car to an empty seat at the rear of the plane, he studied the seventeen-year-old like a hawk, trying to figure out what was so important about her. And when the plane took a nosedive and the pilot managed to right the aircraft, he wondered what role death played in her life. Even as he waited all night outside her hotel room, he couldn't fathom her significance and how her life had intertwined with Dominique's.

Infiniti stepped out of her room early in the morning. Fleet watched her press her back against her door, as if trying not to bump into anyone. But no one was there. She stood in the middle of the hall and called out. She waved her hand before her, as if whisking away a ghost. Fleet narrowed his eyes. Had she caught a glimpse of his energy source? He moved in. He snapped his fingers in front of her face, testing if she could detect him, but she didn't.

He followed her to the lobby for coffee, then into her car to get groceries. He crossed his arms in the backseat and waited for something to happen. He could sense an event was near, but didn't know what kind it would be.

"*Save her,*" the spirit girl whispered in Fleet's head.

Fleet sat forward. *Save her? From what?* He scanned the road ahead of them and behind them. He eyed the trees, the snow, and the mountaintops. Nothing. Yet alarm grew inside of him. He needed Infiniti to get back to the inn. She'd be safer there than on the road. He focused on the electrical system of the car, willing it to short circuit. With lights flashing and static blaring, Infiniti screamed. She slammed on her brakes.

Turn around, he thought. *Go back to your mom. Right the hell now.*

Infiniti hopped out of the car, staring at it as if it had come alive. With his help, it kind of had. And as much as he didn't want to scare the small-framed teen, he needed her to reverse course.

She crept closer to the car. She warned whatever ghost she thought was inside to go away. She slowly got back in the driver's seat. She turned around and started back for the inn, just like he wanted. She reached for her phone, looked at it, and started calling her mother over and over and over until she accidentally dropped the phone.

Dammit, Tiny, come on, Fleet thought, as if he could will Infiniti to get her shit together.

Beyond frustrated with the girl, Fleet sat back. He leaned his head against the seat. Staring at the roof of the car, he was thinking of bailing on her and going back to Houston when the car spun out and plummeted off the highway.

"Son of a bitch!"

The car barreled through branches. Metal creaked and crunched. Glass shattered. He zipped into the seat next to Infiniti. He slammed his hands on the dashboard. He poured every ounce of energy into the car, slowing the plunge as best as he could.

Gritting his teeth, sweat pouring down his forehead, he thought they were almost to the ground when a pop and swish sounded. The strap of Infiniti's seat belt whipped away. Her small frame smashed through the windshield. Fleet catapulted after her. Arm outstretched, he made contact with the back of her wool coat. Clutching the fabric, he pulled her to him. He wrapped his arms around her limp body. With her cradled close in his arms, they slammed against a surface of snow-coated rocks and skidded to a rest.

He clung to her as he caught his breath. He gently eased her on her back. What he saw shocked him to his core. Blood caked her face. A tree branch lodged in her chest, right under her collarbone. Shards of glass were embedded in her neck.

"No, no, no," he whispered.

He placed his fingers under her ear to see if she was alive. Pressing harder, he detected a faint thumping. The spirit girl had said to save Infiniti, that she was important, and right now she was dying. He flung off his leather jacket and got to work.

"Come on, Tiny. Stay with me."

He untangled her legs and arms so that she lay straight. He rubbed his hands together and held them over her face. A stream of sparkling mist oozed from his fingers, coating her face like a liquid mask. Leaving the substance to work on her injuries, he opened her coat all the way and tore her sweater more than it already was, so he could work on her unobstructed. He hovered his hands over her neck and chest and closed his eyes, surveying the damage. He detected broken ribs, bruised lungs, and severe internal bleeding. Although the tree branch sticking into her chest missed any major organs, death appeared imminent.

"Not if I can help it," he seethed.

He released another burst of energy to coat her upper body, taking the time to pour everything he had into healing her. Wiping his brow, he sat back and eyed the unconscious teen.

"Come on, Tiny. Fight."

Fleet eyed her mangled body while an overwhelming sense of guilt flooded him. He had let this happen, and he was pissed at himself. Suddenly, at that moment, nothing else mattered but saving Infiniti.

"She's mine, you know."

A tall guy with short dark hair appeared on the other side of

Infiniti. He was leaning against a tree with crossed arms. "The doll's gonna die no matter what you do, Transhuman."

"Not today, reaper."

"The name is Shade. Shade StormIron. You may have heard of me."

Yeah, he'd heard of the reaper, but didn't want to give him the satisfaction. He ignored his unwanted guest and kept watch over Infiniti.

The reaper let the silence stretch out for a bit. "And you are Fleet, Tavion's right hand. Must suck working for a monster like that. The leader of the Tainted. How can you stand it? Or maybe you love it?"

Fleet's jaw clenched at the thought of Tavion. He couldn't stand it one damn bit, but had resolved to play whatever part was necessary in the war between the Tainted and the Pure.

"Get the hell out of here."

"Hell?" The reaper laughed. "Yeah, I know a thing or two about that place." He moved closer to Infiniti. He watched her for a few seconds before sauntering back over to Fleet. "Seems your efforts have patched her up for the time being. But rest assured, cupcake, her soul is calling for me. This doll's number is due." He licked his lips. "And I'm rather partial to petite brunettes."

Fleet started for the reaper, but he disappeared, leaving Fleet alone with the healing Infiniti. Spent from the exertion, he watched his efforts at work. The tree branch dissolved. The shards of glass disappeared. The blood on her face dissipated. The deep gashes over her forehead, face, and neck started closing. Fleet moved closer to check her pulse when Abigail appeared.

"You did it," Abigail said with a smile.

Fleet picked up his jacket and slipped it on. "Not without a whole hell of a lot of effort. And with that behind me, I'll be heading back to Houston now."

"It's not over," Abigail said.

Footsteps and snapping twigs sounded in the distance. Abigail looked over her shoulder, then back at Fleet. "She'll be transported to a medical center, but she'll be in the wrong time." She reached for Fleet's arm, but her small hand passed right through him. Her Pure energy tingled through his jacket. "She needs to go to 2018. You need to help her get there for something she needs, and then bring her back here to 2012."

Fleet tilted his head. He gazed into her face. "You're a Pure?"

Before he could ask her anything else, the spirit girl disappeared. Two guys burst onto the scene. One had tan skin with short cropped hair. The other had fair skin and blond hair. They couldn't have been much older than thirteen or fourteen. They hurried over to Infiniti and crouched down beside her. Still cloaked by his energy field, Fleet watched to see what they'd do, ready to jump in if needed.

"Oh my God," the guy with blond hair said. "Is she d-d-dead?"

The kid with dark features edged up closer to Infiniti. He put his hand under her nose. "She's alive, but barely." He eyed the wreckage. "It's a miracle."

From his vantage point, Fleet could see Infiniti's wounds were still healing. But with her tattered clothes and the blood that had oozed all over the snow, it made sense for the guys to think she was a lot worse than she was.

"Listen, Joe," the darker kid said. "You need to stay with her while I get help, okay?"

Joe's eyes grew big. "What? Why me, Kase? Why not you?"

"Because I'm faster, that's why."

"B-b-but, Kase, what if she wakes up? What do I do?"

"Keep her calm. She probably won't come to anyway, but I gotta get our dads and Nicholas." Kase put his hands on Joe's shoulders. "I'll hurry, I promise. Okay?"

"Yeah, okay."

"If only I could shift, this would be a lot easier," Kase said, before dashing off through the trees. "Be back soon," he hollered.

Shift? Fleet had no idea what the kid was talking about, but wondered if by chance he was referring to a paranormal shift, one of an animalistic nature.

Fleet scanned the area. Instead of Breckenridge as planned, he and Infiniti and her mom were in the Montrose/Telluride area. After crashing her car, two guys came up from who knew where and one of them talked about shifting like it was no big deal. Suddenly, Fleet knew exactly where they were. He ran his hands through his hair.

"Fucking Havenwood Falls," he muttered to himself.

They were on the outskirts of town, yet close enough for trouble. Transhumans, especially Tavion and the Tainted, were not welcome. The people of the area wanted no part of their civil war. So Transhumans kept their distance. Being here was not good. He knew he'd have to work overtime on his invisibility shield to prevent the supernaturals living in the town from detecting him. He hoped he and Infiniti could get in and out of the area without any problems, because without a doubt the help that would be coming would be from Havenwood Falls. And Havenwood Falls wanted nothing to do with him.

CHAPTER 4

$\mathcal{J}$oe was freaked about being left with a bloodied car crash victim, so he decided to keep busy. If he could keep busy, he wouldn't think about her dying. As a supe, and a descendant of a wolf shifter family, he'd seen a lot of stuff, but nothing like this. But what to do?

He spotted the nearby wreckage and wondered if the girl's stuff was in there. Since his dad was a police officer, Joe figured he should look for evidence. He hoped his dad wouldn't be mad that he and Kase were roaming about outside the Havenwood Falls borders, but he knew he would be.

Walking around carefully, he found grocery items. A package of bagels, cream cheese, bananas, a box of chocolate chip cookies, bottles of water, sport drinks, and several bags of Flamin' Hot Cheetos. Trudging through the snow, hoping to find the girl's purse or phone, he came across the brown sack from the store she must've gone to. He picked it up and inspected it, finding it still intact and without any rips. He thought it strange the paper had come out of the rubble in perfect condition.

Sticking with his distraction plan, he re-sacked the groceries. He put the heavy stuff on the bottom and the lighter stuff on the top. Finishing off with the Cheetos, he thought of his little brother, Boris.

He loved Cheetos, too. Joe was glad Boris hadn't joined his and Kase's afternoon hike. Boris was only eight and still somewhat sheltered from the wolf shifter life. The wreckage and the blood probably would've traumatized him.

With everything he could find in the bag, Joe studied the girl from afar. He gulped, eyeing her still form, thinking she looked lifeless. Her dark clothing and hair stood out in sharp contrast against the snowy background. His heart raced with fear. He wondered if she was dead and thought he should probably check. He had never seen a dead body before and didn't want to, but had to get close. He came from a family of protectors and needed to step into the role.

"Please be okay," he whispered.

Puffs of vapor came out of his mouth as he moved next to her. He had noticed her sweater was torn open the second he and Kase burst onto the scene, but had quickly looked away, because he didn't want to be disrespectful. Plus, her body was covered in blood. Now close to her, he struggled to keep his eyes away from her chest as he held his hand under her nose. Without meaning to, he found himself staring at her black lace bra.

"What are you doing?" he asked himself in horror, his face flushing and his heart thrumming wildly. But then he noticed something. He could actually *see* her bra. He had thought earlier there was too much blood to really see anything. But now, the blood didn't look as red or thick. In fact, it was almost all gone. Or were his eyes playing tricks on him out of stress? He didn't know, but needed to find out.

He leaned in. He examined her chest. He could definitely see her bra and her white skin. He tore his eyes away as a fresh wave of heat gathered in his face.

"Don't be a perv," he said to himself. At almost thirteen, he knew all about that puberty stuff. Sometimes it was a struggle for him to keep his eyes where they needed to be whenever a pretty girl was around. But this was different. He needed to make sure the girl was still alive.

He drew in a series of deep breaths. "Be cool and help," he said to himself.

He brought his attention back to the girl and waited for movement. Her chest rose ever so slightly, then fell. "Thank God," he sighed with relief.

He studied her face. Even though crisscrossing cuts laced her cheeks and forehead, he thought she was beautiful. Petite, with delicate features and long dark hair, she was probably one of the most gorgeous girls he'd ever seen. He wondered where she was from and how the heck she had crashed her car off the side of the mountain. He also couldn't believe her injuries didn't look as bad as when he and Kase first saw her. Or maybe most of her injuries were internal. Or maybe she was a supe. No matter what she was or how she got there or what may or may not have been happening to her wounds, his worry over her condition elevated with each thought.

"Please don't die, okay?" he said with a nervous laugh.

He reached for her coat with trembling hands, wanting to cover her up, when she stirred. A moan came out of her. Her eyes fluttered open. A series of groans escaped her lips as she tried to sit up. He put his hands on her shoulders in an effort to steady her.

"It's okay. You're okay. Try not to move."

Easing back down, she looked about in a daze before she noticed him. She blinked, forcing herself to bring his face into focus.

"Who are you?" she asked.

While he was locked in a stare with her, a feeling struck Joe in the pit of his stomach. Strange and unfamiliar, it grew inside of him. He tried to make sense of the sensation while at the same time trying to form words to answer her.

"Where am I?" the girl asked. She tried to move, and a yelp escaped her lips.

Joe steadied her again. "My name is Joe. You were in an accident. My friend and I found you. He went to get help and should be back soon."

He watched the girl look around, dazed and out of it.

"You really shouldn't move," he warned, concern for her safety taking over his thoughts. He took her hand and held it. It was delicate, small, and cold. Since he hadn't had his first shift yet, he couldn't warm her skin with his own. He hated that he still hadn't made the change, but knew it would come soon. At almost thirteen, he looked more like fifteen or sixteen. If only he could help her somehow.

He thought of pulling off his sweatshirt and draping it over her for extra warmth. He'd started to release her hand when she gripped him with surprising strength. She held him in place.

"Don't leave me," she pleaded.

"I'm not," he blurted, wanting to comfort her, his protective instincts kicking into high gear. "I was gonna take off my sweatshirt and put it over you. It'll help keep you warm. Is that okay?"

"O-k-k-kay," she managed to choke out.

He carefully moved her hand to the ground, as if it were made of glass. He tugged off his sweatshirt in one fluid motion. He spread it out over her chest and arms.

"There," he said. "Is that better?"

Her eyes had welled with tears. She couldn't speak, so settled on a nod.

He scooted closer. "I'm right here and I'm not—" His sentence cut short as his voice pitched low and then high again. *Damn puberty.* He cleared his throat. "I'm not leaving you."

He thought about the time he broke his arm when he was little. He was climbing a tree and lost his footing on a high branch. He had hurtled to the ground and snapped his arm in two. Kase was there to calm him until his dad arrived and took him to the medical center. Kase told him funny stories to occupy his mind throughout the ordeal. He thought of doing the same with the girl, but didn't know what to say.

"So, uh, what's your name?" She didn't respond, her eyes looking freaked out and panicky. "Where are you from?"

Her eyes darted around the area, taking in the mangled car and downed trees. Tears spilled down her cheeks. It was as if she realized for the first time what had happened to her.

"I crashed." And then she whispered, "Cheetos."

"Cheetos?" As crazy as it seemed, he wondered if she wanted some.

"Are you hungry?" He eyed the grocery bag not too far away. "Do you want me to—?"

She gripped his hand. She pulled him close. He stared into her big brown eyes, wanting nothing more than to wipe away her tears and tell her everything would be okay. And then he thought of her bra, and her skin. He pushed the image of her exposed chest from his mind, trying to focus on helping her.

She brought him in with a desperate and scared look on her face. "I'm dying."

Blood had oozed into the snow, forging a path through the white terrain like a liquid fire. With so much blood on her clothing and around her, he thought she might be right, but didn't want to say so.

"No, you're fine."

"There's so much I haven't done yet. And now it's too late." Fresh tears flooded her eyes. She looked away from him for a second before looking back at him. "Joe, I'm going to tell you I love you, and I want you to say it back."

"What?" A wave of emotion he'd never felt before enveloped him. His skin tingled. His palms grew sweaty. His stomach dropped. The image of her skin and bra popped in his mind.

"Please," she said, propping herself up with a groan. "Do this for me before . . ." Her lip trembled. "Before I go."

"Uh, okay," he agreed, feeling immense sorrow for the beautiful girl and wanting to do whatever she asked.

"I love you," she breathed out.

Everything around him amplified. He saw her more clearly than ever, his senses sharpened like never before. Deep rich brown hair and eyes, perfectly fair skin that reminded him of milk. Even the hue of her cuts looked fluorescent and magical.

"I, uh, love you, too."

His muscles tensed. His jaw clenched. Every internal organ started throbbing. He dropped the girl's hand. He backed away.

"Oh, no," he uttered.

Starting with his feet and cascading all the way up to his neck, his bones broke, then healed, then broke again. His teeth grew to razor sharp points, slicing through his gums. His fingernails jutted out, forming thick nails that could kill with a swipe. With a yell that turned into a howl, fur replaced his skin until he was on all fours.

A wolf now, he felt beyond incredible. Strong, energized, and electric. He considered running away from the girl because he didn't want to scare her, but he also didn't want to leave her alone. He had to protect her until Kase and the others arrived.

"Stay!" she called out, helping him make up his mind. She was propped up on her forearms, taking him in with astonished eyes. She held out her arm. "It's okay."

In this truest form of himself, he found her beauty magnified. She even looked as if the cuts lacing her body had started to fade, though he thought it was impossible. Maybe his new wolf vision was playing tricks on him. He approached with caution. Head slightly down, tail swishing back and forth, he came to a halt beside her.

"J-J-Joe? You're a w-w-wolf?" she asked between chattering teeth, the cold taking over her reflexes. "A b-b-beautiful w-w-white w-w-wolf? Or am I d-d-dying and s-s-s-seeing things?"

He nudged his head under her hand, letting her know he was real. Sensing she was relaxed and at ease with him in this form, and feeling how freezing she was, he curled up next to her to share his body heat. She moved her hand slowly down his back, working her fingers through his thick fur. He detected her skin warming, her muscles relaxing. She nestled next to him. The vibration of her heartbeat settled into a strong and steady beat until she finally fell asleep.

After what seemed like forever, but couldn't have been more than an hour, Joe detected movement in the brush. Ears in the radar position and snout in the air, he sensed his dad, Sheriff Ric Kasun, and EMT Nicholas Jordan approaching, their usual stealth mode overtaken by the dragging and banging of something in tow.

Faint at first, the din grew louder until two wolves—his dad and Sheriff Ric—and a mountain lion—Nicholas—emerged onto the scene. Nicholas pulled behind him a stretcher with a bag strapped to the middle. The three morphed to human form.

"Well," Nicholas said. "Look who made the change."

Joe huffed but stayed by the girl's side. He watched his dad, Sheriff Ric, and Nicholas put on the clothes that had been stuffed in the pack and tied to the stretcher. His dad walked over to him and the girl.

"Son, that must've been a pretty intense experience." He patted Joe firmly on the head. "You've done good work here, but now you need to step aside so Nicholas can do his job."

"Thanks, Ivan," Nicholas said.

Joe knew his dad was right. He got up and moved away, but stayed close and in wolf form. Sitting back on his haunches, he kept a keen eye on his charge.

Nicholas removed Joe's outstretched sweatshirt from the girl. He made a visual assessment with a furrowed brow.

"This doesn't make sense," he muttered. "Ric, Ivan, you too, Joe. Come look at this."

Everyone moved closer to see what Nicholas meant. Joe tried not to stare at the girl's plunging lace bra and instead focused on the spot where Nicholas pointed.

"There's clear evidence of a wound here," Nicholas explained. "Right below her clavicle. The skin is red and bruised. There's blood everywhere. But there's no puncture."

"An injury with no injury?" Sheriff Ric rubbed his chin. "That doesn't make sense."

"Maybe she's a supe," his dad suggested.

Nicholas kept a perplexed look on his face. "Maybe. It does seem as if her wounds have been . . . healed? Or were never there?" He eyed Joe. "Did you see actual punctures?"

Joe huffed and nodded his assent. He had seen the cuts, and remembered her looking way worse when he first came upon the scene.

His dad and Sheriff Ric kicked into officer mode. They scanned the forest, peering about. Joe wondered what they were looking for.

"You see anything, Ivan?" Sheriff Ric asked his dad. "Anything to indicate anyone else could have been here?"

His dad swept the landscape with laser focus. "Nope, I don't." He went up to Joe. "Son, do you see anything?"

In wolf form, Joe would be able to see and smell things the others couldn't in human form. He perked up his ears. He pointed his nose in different directions and sniffed about. He moved in a circle studying every inch of the woods around them, but didn't detect anything. He huffed and shook his head no. He was as confused as they were about the girl's miraculous recovery.

Nicholas dragged the stretcher over. "Whatever is going on, we need to get her to the med center, and quick. The temps are dropping fast. We can figure out more when we get her there."

Joe watched his dad pick up the sack of groceries. He poked through the contents. "No phone or purse?" his dad asked him.

Joe shook his head.

"I'll bring the evidence," his dad said to Sheriff Ric.

"Nicholas and I have the stretcher," Sheriff Ric responded.

On three, Sheriff Ric and Nicholas carefully lifted the girl and set her on the portable stretcher. Nicholas went to his pack and pulled out a thick blanket. He covered the girl from her feet all the way up to her chin.

"Alright," Nicholas said. "Let's get her out of here."

Joe watched Sheriff Ric and Nicholas carry the girl away. His dad followed behind with the grocery sack. Joe filed in after them. They painstakingly carried her up the bank and to the nearest road, where Nicholas's ambulance was parked. Joe watched as the three slid the girl in the back.

"We'll see you at the clinic, son," his dad said, leaving him to follow them to Havenwood Falls on all fours. "Make sure you get out of these parts and back in the city limits quick. We'll talk later about why you and Kase were out here in the first place."

At that moment, breaking the rules and hiking outside of Havenwood Falls didn't matter to Joe. As the flashing lights faded away, Joe could only think about the girl and the emotions she had stirred in him. She said she loved him because she thought she was dying, and he had said it back. He wondered if it was the words that prompted his shift, or her skin, or her lace bra. Probably it was all of it.

Either way, he vowed never to talk about it with his dad or Kase or anyone. They'd never understand.

CHAPTER 5

leet didn't want to witness Infiniti's emotional interaction with the kid, didn't want to hear her pour her heart out because she thought she was dying, so he kept his distance. And when the pack of supernaturals, two wolf shifters and one mountain lion shifter, arrived and morphed into human form, he moved even farther away.

Still cloaked and crouching down near a cluster of snow-laden bushes, he kept a keen eye on the group. After a quick inspection, and talk over Infiniti's missing wounds, they strapped her to the stretcher, wrapped her in a blanket, and loaded her into an ambulance. Only the kid remained, still in wolf form, but he soon raced off after them.

Finally alone, Fleet stepped out onto the road. He examined the space all around him. He looked up at the gray sky.

"Now would be a really good time for you to show yourself."

He waited for the spirit girl to appear, but she didn't. Her words repeated in his head.

She needs to go to 2018.

He thought of what Tavion had said back at the penthouse.

She's important.

He faced the direction the ambulance had driven and started formulating a plan. Lock on to Infiniti's signature, go to wherever the ambulance was taking her, whisk her to 2018, and hope the spirit girl would appear and tell them what to do. He just hoped he could do whatever needed to be done before any supes in the town could figure out what was happening. The last thing he needed was to start something deadly with the locals.

Moving from the road to a nearby cluster of trees, he waited a bit to make sure Infiniti would have plenty of time to arrive at her destination. With her wounds more than likely gone by her arrival, she'd be placed in a room and kept there until she would awake. He needed to time his arrival perfectly, or everything would be for naught.

Eyeing the setting sun, he thought of Infiniti. He feared for her safety, but he also felt something else—sorrow. She didn't deserve to get caught up in his mess. At seventeen, she had so much to live for, yet here she was, fighting for her survival, and she didn't even know it. He was tired as hell at all the death in his life but resolved right then and there to get Infiniti out of Havenwood Falls alive.

Stars started sprinkling the wintry sky. He thought enough time had passed for Infiniti to be in an optimal location. He doubled his cloaking efforts to avoid detection in the town. He rubbed his hands together, blew into them, and placed them on the snowy ground. He pictured Infiniti—long dark hair, big brown eyes, petite features, and important.

"Go to her," he whispered.

Gray vapor poured out of his hands. The warm tingling mist pooled around his feet, swirling beneath him like a whirlpool. He slipped into weightlessness, then found himself on solid ground.

Crouched down, he surveyed his new surroundings. He appeared to be in a small dark hospital room. He rose to his feet and spotted Infiniti. She was lying on a twin-sized bed tucked under a white sheet, fast asleep. Her face and hair had been cleaned. He could see that she still wore her red sweater, but it wasn't ripped or bloodied anymore. He thought someone in the clinic must've magically repaired her clothes. A light nasal snore filled the air. He spotted a bag on a chair in the corner of the room and recognized the fur from her boots peeking over the edge. He grabbed the bag and placed it on her legs. He put his hand on her shoulder.

"Okay," he muttered. "Let's see what's in store for us in 2018, Tiny."

Focusing on the exact same place, but a different year, his energy stream oozed out like a fog. It swirled around them like a slow-churning funnel cloud. The phenomenon picked up speed, and Fleet felt the floor drop from below him. A few seconds passed before he met solid surface under his feet.

He looked around and saw that he was in the same place with Infiniti, but he could sense they were in a different time. The walls were the same plain white; the bed and side table identical. Only the chair in the corner had changed from the one that had been there six years earlier. Fleet studied Infiniti's sleeping form. He placed the bag back on the chair. He stepped back. He waited for her to wake up, wondering what would happen next.

CHAPTER 6

*I*nfiniti heard a soft whisper. It floated around her head like a breeze. Cool and inviting, it comforted her while she slept, until, eventually, it didn't want her sleeping anymore.

"Wake up," the voice urged. "Now!"

She swatted at the source, irritated at being woken up, yet peeled her eyes open anyway. "Okay, okay, sheesh. I'm getting up."

Rubbing her head, she was wondering how late she had overslept and what test she was going to miss when she noticed her walls weren't purple anymore. Even her black comforter had been replaced with a flimsy white sheet. And that's when reality gripped her. She wasn't home. She hadn't overslept. She wasn't going to be late to school. She was in Colorado, she had been driving, and . . .

She sat up with a jolt. The sudden motion rocked her head. Stars littered her vision. She moaned, easing herself back down. When the twinkling faded, she sat back up with caution.

"Holy shit," she whispered to herself.

The overpowering smell of hand sanitizer and bleach invaded her nostrils. She scanned the small room. She was on a twin-sized bed with raised bed rails. To the right was a closed door, to the left was a small window, and in the corner was a chair with a plastic bag. No one was around, so who was telling her to wake up? Or was the voice part of some weird dream?

"Where am I?"

A tray next to her held an oversized plastic cup with a lid and a straw. Seeing the cup prompted her to realize how dry her mouth was. She took the cup and sipped, yet nothing came out of the straw. She lifted the cup and shook it, but it was empty.

"Really?" she mumbled.

She set the cup down with shaky hands and swallowed but didn't have enough spit to coat her throat. Feeling drained and empty, she sat there for a second while her brain processed her situation. Then realization hit her like a brick. Her car had swerved, she lost control, but what had happened after that?

She rubbed her head, trying to piece together the events from the swerve to now. She thought she must've crashed, but couldn't remember any of the details. Her body ached all over, and her muscles felt sore and stiff. She wondered how bad her injuries were. She brought her fingers to her face, moving them around inch by inch, but her skin felt fine. She patted her arms and then her chest and thighs. There was no indication of breaks or anything like that, even though she felt as if she'd been run over by a train.

"Mom," she whispered to herself. Her heart lurched at the thought of her mom at the inn, worried and scared. Her eyes met the bag on the chair. Her stuff had to be in there, including her phone.

She pushed down on the bed rail, forcing it to collapse, and then peeled off the white bed sheet. She examined her clothes. She was wearing the same outfit she had put on back at the inn. Despite a few wrinkles here and there, her clothes looked fine. She swung her legs over the side of the bed and stood. She shuffled over to the bag. Peering in, she saw her boots and nothing else. No wallet. No phone. She patted the back pocket of her jeans, hoping to find it there, but didn't. There wasn't even a phone in the room.

"Great."

Thinking she needed to get out of there, she pulled on her boots. She stepped out into the hallway, discovering she was in what looked like a house converted to a clinic. An empty clinic. A little spooky, even. The lights were dimmed, and not a sound could be heard.

"Hello?" She waited for a response. "Anyone here?"

Making her way down the hall and out the door, she stepped outside. A cold blast hit her face. Snow flurries floated around her. She crossed her arms and held them snug to her body, wondering what had happened to her new coat. She loved that coat.

Turning back around, she faced the building and saw that she had stepped out of a white house with blue trim. A sign over the door read *Medical Center*. As she surveyed her situation, a yummy smell of greasy goodness drifted her way. Her stomach growled. Her eyes followed the scent. Down the street she spotted a shopping center with a fast food restaurant in front of it. Outside a vintage neon sign blinked *Burger Bar*.

"Oh, thank God."

She hurried for the burger place, hoping she'd find someone to take pity on the lost girl from Houston who was starving and needed to use a phone.

The cute restaurant with a black-and-white-checkered floor bustled with activity. Lively Christmas music played from an antique-looking jukebox. Christmas decorations adorned each wall. She made her way to the back so she could scope things out. Eyeing the crowd, she wondered whom she should approach for help. Her attention landed on the TV in the back of the room. The news was on. The reporter was talking to the obnoxious rich guy with the hideous comb-over from *The Apprentice*. The guy that fired everyone.

"Huh," she muttered to herself. "Wonder what that wacko is up to and why he's in the White House."

She was trying to make out the interview conversation when someone tapped her shoulder. She turned around and saw a guy her age. Tall and slender, he had short-cropped blond hair and piercing hazel eyes. He sported a blue letterman's jacket with white and silver accents. He tilted his head to the side and stared at her with a slightly parted mouth.

"You're the girl."

"I'm the girl?" She had no idea who he was or what he was talking about, not that she minded too much. He was gorgeous.

His eyes scanned her face, roamed her body, landed on her boobs, and then returned to her face. Astonishment mixed with joy took over his expression.

"You're okay. And you're . . . here."

"Yes, I'm here, and I seem to be fine."

She relaxed her stance, grateful to have found a friendly person who must've seen her being brought into the medical center. A hot person at that. He was sure to have a phone she could use, and money to buy her some food.

"Do you happen to have a—"

"How did you get here?" He got up close, as if her answer was some sort of secret. "Where have you been?"

She gave him a curious look. She pointed in the direction of the medical center. "Well, um, I've been at that medical center house down the street, and I walked over here."

Eyeing the guy, she thought maybe there was something wrong with him, especially since she had a history of attracting weirdos. She started backing away.

"Excuse me," she said, clearing her throat. "But I need to go."

Before she could turn away, a memory blasted through her. It shook her through to her core, rooting her in place. She was lying on the snowy ground, bleeding. A guy was with her. He looked like the guy before her. Same blond hair, same hazel eyes, but younger. She thought she was dying. She had asked him to say he loved her. And then he had transformed into a white wolf.

Her mouth dropped. A wave of goose bumps dashed across her skin. She backed away a little. He was the same guy, but older.

"You're . . . the . . . the . . . the wolf." Tears sprang to her eyes. "I thought I was dying. You stayed with me, and I asked you to—"

"Shh," he said. His warm hand took her cold one, and he pulled her into the nearest empty booth.

Heat filled her cheeks as she remembered every second of her encounter with him. She was horrified, embarrassed, and freaked out all at the same time. How was she okay? How did he look older? Was he really a wolf? And why the hell had she asked him to say he loved her?

"I can't believe it's you," he whispered.

A guy with tan skin and dark hair came up to them. "Dude, Joe, there you are. I was looking for—" The guy took a good look at Infiniti. He dropped his phone, and it clanked on the metal table. "Holy shit, the girl."

The guy across from her said again, "Yeah, the girl."

Coming completely unglued, she said, "Yeah, I'm the freakin' girl!"

This time both guys shushed her, looking around to make sure no one had heard them.

"Somebody'd better tell me what the hell is going on before I start screaming!"

The blond guy held up his hands, as if to calm her down. "I will, I promise." He eyed his friend. "Give us a sec, okay?"

"Yeah, sure," the dark-haired guy said, getting his phone and leaving with a shocked look on his face.

He returned to a group by the counter, but Infiniti didn't pay them any attention. She couldn't. Her mind reeled at the pieces of her ordeal filtering back into her memory. Throbbing pain. Splattered blood. Shards of glass. The guy looking younger and transforming into a wolf. What the hell was happening?

"Who are you?" the guy whispered.

"I'm Infiniti. I'm from Houston. Who are you?"

"I'm Joe, and I'm from here. Havenwood Falls."

"Havenwood Falls?"

"Yeah." He leaned over the table. "The town close to where you crashed. You were transported to the medical center." He moved in even closer. "You disappeared."

She stared at him in disbelief. She pressed her back against the booth. It took her a minute to find her voice. "I what?"

"You vanished. We searched for you for days. Months, even. With no leads, we had to give up."

Her hands folded and unfolded on her lap. Her mind raced. "I crashed. I woke up, and I walked over here."

"You woke up? As in, just now?"

"Yes."

"*Now* now?"

"Yes. Like ten minutes ago now."

His brows stitched together. He rubbed his chin. "So what happened to the last six years?"

Six years?

She examined his face. He most definitely looked six years older, but her car crash had happened that day. So that would be impossible. But then she thought of all the sci-fi movies she'd seen, and all her supernatural paraphernalia at home—her Ouija board, the spiritual cards her neighbor Jan had given her. She was a believer in all things unexplained, but had something otherworldly really happened to her? As in, for real?

Her hands trembled. She shivered. "It's 2018?"

"Yeah, it's 2018."

Her gut clenched. Every sound in the restaurant faded as horror and shock crowded her senses. Panic soared through her veins. "Give me your phone."

"What?"

"Your phone. Please. Give it to me."

He handed her the sleekest phone she'd ever seen. She pressed the home button, desperate to call her mom, but nothing happened. Staring at it, she had no idea how to get it to work. He motioned for her to give it back.

"I need to put my thumb on there."

"Your thumb?'

She held it out. He placed his thumb on it and the device sprang to life.

"Holy shit, I am in the future. I really am."

She stared at all the bright apps, not really sure how to make a call, or even if she *should* make a call. She had wanted to call her mom, but her mom was in the past now, and she was in the future, and there was the whole time-space-continuum thing to consider. She had no idea what to do. Her throat clogged with tears.

Joe slid out of his side of the booth and scooted in next to her. He put his arm around her and held her close. "Hey, it's okay. I'm here. I'm not gonna leave you."

She pulled away and stared at him. Every moment on the mountainside came back to her in a whoosh—the bitter cold on her face, the pain in her body, the blood trickling from her wounds. All of it.

"You said those words to me on the mountainside, when I thought I was dying."

She didn't want to lose it in front of a stranger, but a lone tear slipped out onto her cheek. He wiped it away. "I know. I meant it then, and I mean it now. I will help you, I promise."

His reassuring words started to comfort her but fell short. She was stuck in a time and place she didn't belong. And even though she had a gorgeous guy by her side, all she wanted to do was go home.

CHAPTER 7

*J*oe couldn't believe his eyes. The girl from the crash who had said she loved him was standing in Burger Bar. The last time he'd seen her was six years ago. He remembered every second of their encounter because it had sparked his first shift. He had even felt called to her, but was so young at the time, he didn't realize it. Her long dark hair, her bloodstained clothes, her fair skin, her lace bra, every word she had spoken—it had repeated in his mind at least a million times over the years. And now, miraculously, she stood in the back of his favorite burger place, chewing her bottom lip and staring at the TV. An overwhelming sense of needing to protect her had kicked in back then, and stirred again inside of him.

How is she here?

He and a handful of friends had finished their last final and were celebrating with burgers and shakes when suddenly nothing mattered but the girl. He left his friends at the counter and went to her. With each approaching step, he marveled at the fact that she looked exactly the same, minus the injuries. She even wore the same clothing, yet her wardrobe wasn't torn or stained anymore.

Fumbling for what to say, and resisting the overwhelming urge to wrap her up in a bear hug, he settled on an awkward intro.

"You're the girl."

Talking to her, he found out her name was Infiniti and that she was from Houston. She remembered the crash and that he had shifted into a wolf. But what took her awhile to understand was that the crash and his transformation had happened in 2012.

Her hands trembled. She shivered as if she'd been standing outside in a blizzard.

"It's 2018?"

"Yeah," he said, wanting to help her but not knowing how. "It's 2018."

Sitting in a booth at the back of the restaurant, she asked to borrow his phone so she could call her mom. It was the strangest thing to see her stare at the device, completely unable to use it. A beautiful girl, out of time, and all alone. Doing his best to comfort her, he sat next to her and hugged her, saying he wouldn't leave her, but what could he do? She didn't belong in Havenwood Falls, let alone 2018. And then he thought of the wards. Her presence was sure to trigger them. He was about to tell her they should get out of there when his phone beeped. It was a text from his dad.

Dad: Sheriff Kasun has reinstated the APB for the girl from the crash who went missing six years ago. If you see anything strange, let me know ASAP. And come home right after you eat. Something is not right in the town.

Crap, this wasn't good. Not at all. He didn't want to be rude to the girl, especially since she looked like she was seconds from breaking down, but he needed more info from his dad.

"My dad is texting," he said to her. "Gotta text back real quick."

Me: Huh? Not right with the town?

Dad: Lyra Beaumont and others in the Luna Coven have recognized an energy shift, same as the one they felt when the girl went missing in 2012. Probably nothing, but stay sharp, ok?

Joe's heart hammered against his chest as he read his dad's text a few times. The message, combined with his dad's recent overprotectiveness, made his gut tighten. He replied with a simple *OK*, then stashed his phone in his back pocket. Scanning the faces in the restaurant, he thought he should get the girl out of there before they were spotted. There were too many people around, and he wanted to protect her from whatever minions the Court of the Sun and the Moon would surely be sending her way. Even if it meant his ass, he wanted whatever time he could get with her. His dad would have to get over it.

"Let's go someplace where we can be alone and talk."

He started to get out of the booth, but she pulled him back down. "After we get some food and drink, if that's okay. I'm starving."

He was starving, too. "Good idea," he said, thinking her hunger meant she was calming down a bit.

He spotted Kase getting his order, and an idea came to him. "Hold on a sec," he said to Infiniti.

Joe approached the counter, grabbed a to-go bag, and started stuffing Kase's usual double order in the bag. Two burgers, two fries and a bottle of soda. Perfect for him and Infiniti.

"Dude," Kase whispered, so focused on the girl he didn't even mind his food being stolen. "What is going on? I just got a text from my dad."

"I know. I got a text from my dad, too. You didn't say anything, did you?"

"Nah, wanted to talk to you first." Kase peered over Joe's shoulder. "How is she here?"

"I don't know, but I'm gonna find out."

Kase pulled him close. "I see it in your eyes, dude." He lowered his voice even more. "Are you called to her?"

Deep affection for the girl had budded in him back when he was twelve and never left him. Back then, he didn't know what it was. He had also never mentioned it to anyone, and didn't plan on it now. He held up the bag of food. "I'll pay you back for this."

"That's fine, but Joe," Kase looked around the place, "we need to tell our dads that she's here, before the Court gets involved, and we're grounded for life."

"I know, and I will, but I want to talk to her first." He eyed his best friend for a few seconds, giving him the *I'm serious* look. "Okay?"

"Yeah, okay," Kase said with an exasperated grunt. "May as well warn her about the interrogation that's sure to come. If our dads know something is up, then Addie must be losing her shit right now. She's been on the warpath with everything going on, you know, with that Harper girl being missing and everything."

Joe clasped Kase on the shoulder. "Good idea. I'll give her a heads up."

Joe went back to Infiniti, still not believing she was right in front of him. "We're all set with food for two." Eyeing her outfit, he took off his jacket and handed it to her. "But you're gonna need this. It's really cold outside." As a wolf shifter, he didn't need protection from the elements like regular humans. She slipped it on, and it engulfed her petite frame. He smiled. "It's a tad too big on you."

The lighthearted moment erased the worry lines on her face. "It's perfect. Thanks, Joe. But why are we leaving? And where are we going? And just so you know, I'm trying really hard not to lose it," she said with a nervous laugh.

His heart swelled with tenderness and sympathy for the girl, and he knew right then and there he'd do anything for her. His mind scrambled to figure out where they could go when he spotted his high school through the window. It was late, so nobody would be there, except maybe the janitor. He thought he could find an unlocked door pretty easily.

"I know the perfect place. Come on."

With the bag of food and drink in one hand, and Infiniti's dainty hand in the other, they left Burger Bar.

"My school is right over there." He indicated with his chin the three-story red-brick building with an arched doorway. Luckily, a few lights were still on. They hurried to the front entrance, rushing to get out of the snowfall, and found the door unlocked.

Stepping inside, Infiniti looked around the dark hallway.

"Why does it feel like we're hiding?" she asked in a hushed voice.

He continued down the hallway. "I'll explain as soon as we get to the room." He stopped at a door at the end of the hall. He peered through the glass panels to see inside and saw that it was all clear.

Once inside, he turned on a small lamp at the back. "This is the art room. We can hang here while we figure things out."

He sat at a long wooden table and watched Infiniti roam about for a few seconds, eyeing the hanging artwork.

"Are you an artist?" she asked.

"Me? Nah. I picked this room because of the tables. I'm into sports."

She sat across from him as he emptied the contents of their to-go order on long sheets of drawing paper. He kept watching her expressions, thinking she was probably in shock or something. Keeping quiet, waiting for her to process everything, he started eating. She did, too. He stopped himself from gulping his food down like he normally did, and chewed at a slow pace. He was searching for the right thing to say to her when she started the conversation.

"I . . . time traveled." She set her fry down. "And you . . . are a wolf."

"A wolf shifter," he explained. "There's a big difference."

"A wolf shifter," she repeated in a low voice. She moved her food around on the paper, as if trying to figure out if she still wanted to eat. "Is this for real? Is this really happening?" She stared off in the distance. "Maybe I'm in a coma." She pinched her arm.

"You're not in a coma, I promise." Images of her fair skin and black lace bra entered his brain. He forced himself to focus on her big brown eyes instead. "And yes, this is really happening."

"And the wolf thing?"

"Wolf shifter thing," he clarified. He thought of the prime directive of Havenwood Falls to keep all things supernatural hidden. But since she was a time traveler, and had already seen him shift, he thought it best to be honest with her about the town.

He rubbed the back of his neck. "This whole town, Havenwood Falls, is filled with supernatural beings."

Her mouth fell open, closed, then fell open again. "Stuff like that isn't real," she finally said. "I mean, if it were real, people would know about it. Like, this place would've been all over the news."

"I can assure you, it's real. This town is a safe haven for us. And when people leave, they forget everything." A pang of sorrow at the idea of her leaving and forgetting him shut his brain off for a second. He paused for a few seconds before going on. "It's the way the town and the people living in it are protected. It's how we stay hidden." He waited for her to say something, but she didn't. He decided to continue so he could prepare her for whomever the Court of the Sun and Moon would be sending their way. "And when people come here without being registered, there's an investigation."

Her eyes took on a spark of recognition. "Someone is going to come investigate me?" She swallowed. "So I'm like in trouble or something?"

"No. I mean, yes, but it's not bad. That's why I brought you here, so I could tell you, and also, you know, so we could talk."

He wanted to tell her so much more, but didn't know how to begin or what to say. She had been a part of his life for six years. He had been called to her, and the idea of her being in any kind of jeopardy had him on red alert. Secretly he hoped she wouldn't be able to get back to her home. He wanted her to stay.

Feeling a pull toward her, he moved closer. "Infiniti, back at the crash when you said you loved me, I felt something for you." He waited for a bit before continuing. "I know I was young, and it may sound unbelievable, but—" He stopped short of revealing his attachment to her and instead said, "You're special."

Infiniti blushed. "I am?"

"Yes, you are."

She gazed at him for a while. "It doesn't make any sense at all, but I kind of feel something for you, too," she said. "It's like our experience on that mountain bonded us in a way."

"I know," he said.

He reached across the table and took her hand, wondering if his bond with her sparked some sort of return in affection. He hoped so. He stared into her sweet and innocent eyes. Without even knowing what he was doing, he leaned across the table, and she did, too. Their lips almost met when Joe's spine tingled with alarm. The air in the room changed. He jumped to his feet, ready to shift, when a guy materialized out of thin air. Tall, with dark jeans and a leather jacket, he held a ball of light in his hand. He aimed it straight at him.

"I'm not here to hurt you," the menacing stranger said to Joe before he could shift. "But I need Infiniti."

Infiniti was on her feet now, looking at the guy with shock. "Uh . . . I don't know who you are, but I'm not going anywhere with you."

Joe moved Infiniti behind him. "I suggest you get out of here," he growled, "before I—"

"Shift to wolf form? I've seen it. Six years ago at the wreckage when you came upon Infiniti."

"What?" Infiniti whispered. "You were there?"

Joe's mind picked apart the afternoon he had stumbled upon Infiniti. He had combed the area in wolf form. His eyes, ears, and nose hadn't detected anyone around. Even his dad, Nicholas, and Sheriff Ric hadn't sensed anyone.

"If you were there, I would've known."

The stranger looked impatient. He gritted his teeth. "I don't have time for this. Someone is coming, and I need to get Infiniti out of here. Now step aside or I'll have to make you." The stranger kept his energy ball at the ready, his eyes narrowed with determination. "You don't want me to make you."

Joe's phone beeped, interrupting the deadly face-off between himself and the stranger. Over and over it dinged with messages. It even rang. Joe knew the guy was right. Something was happening, and someone was trying to warn him.

Assessing the guy with his heightened senses, he quickly came to the conclusion that he meant them no harm. He relaxed his stance, but stayed close to Infiniti. He took her hand, lacing his fingers with hers.

"If you take her, you're taking me, too."

Boots pounded down the corridor. Joe detected the stride of Sheriff Ric and two females. Still gripping Infiniti's hand, he went up to the guy. Unafraid of him or his weapon, he growled, "Those are my people coming, and you'd better not hurt them."

47

CHAPTER 8

*E*ven though Fleet thought he could trust the wolf shifter, he wasn't so sure the people coming down the hallway would trust him. One look at him, and they'd know he was one of the Tainted, Tavion's second-in-command, because he had played the role for over a century. Supernaturals the world over knew him, feared him, and kept their distance. Yet here he was, in the hidden mecca of supernatural suburbia where supes lived with humans. He wondered why the spirit girl wanted him and Infiniti to come here.

The energy ball warmed his hand and sizzled with power. If seen as the aggressor, he'd be attacked and would have to respond. The last thing he wanted to do was kill innocents. Plus, he knew the lovestruck kid standing before him would pounce. He sensed the protectiveness he had for Infiniti.

Footsteps thudded closer. He could hear the swishing of clothing. He cursed under his breath, then let the power in his hand dissolve. He eyed the kid glued to Infiniti's side.

"Listen up, Joe. I'm not going to hurt them. Trust me on that. But we do things my way. Got it?"

Before Joe could formulate a response, the classroom door swung open. Fleet zipped in front of Infiniti and her newfound defender. He let loose a stream of energy at a man and two women. The gray mist shot out like a laser beam, freezing the trio in place.

Infiniti covered her mouth. "Holy shit," she mumbled through her fingers.

She and Joe approached the mannequin-like bodies. Joe waved his hand in front of the faces of the frozen.

"Are they okay?"

Fleet came up beside Joe. "They're fine. Who's in charge?"

Joe pointed at the dark-haired man. "That's Sheriff Kasun. He's kind of in charge."

"Kind of?"

"Well, it's complicated."

"Who's everyone else?"

Joe pointed at the older woman with shoulder-length brown hair dressed in gypsy attire. "That's Lyra Beaumont." He pointed at the younger woman next to her. Wearing dark-rimmed glasses and dressed like she could be in a rock band, she resembled the taller woman. "That's her daughter, Addie." Joe looked worried and guilty. "I guess they're looking for me." He eyed Infiniti. "And you."

"Me? They don't even know me or that I'm here."

Joe ran his fingers through his hair. "They had an idea. My dad is a police officer. He texted me while I was in Burger Bar. He wanted to know if I had seen you, the missing girl from the crash six years ago."

Infiniti shot him a look. "Why didn't you tell me?"

Before Joe could explain, Fleet cut in. "It doesn't matter. We're here, and this is happening. And I need to talk to the sheriff."

Joe pulled Infiniti, and together they backed up a little. "Okay, but he's not gonna be happy."

"Well neither am I," Fleet muttered.

Fleet approached Sheriff Kasun. He laid his fingers on the man's forehead. A spark connected at his skin, and Sheriff Kasun sprang to life. With a blink, he went for his gun, but Fleet beat him to it. He drew it from the holster with lightning speed.

"Sheriff Kasun, my name is Fleet, and I mean you no harm." Fleet showed him the gun, then slowly handed it back as a sign of trust. "But I will fight back if I'm attacked, and I don't want to do that."

The sheriff narrowed his piercing blue eyes at Fleet. He took the gun and put it back in its place. "I don't want you to do that, either." He scanned the still bodies of Lyra and Addie before examining Joe and Infiniti. "Joe, are you and your friend okay?"

"Yes. Her name's Infiniti, and we're fine," Joe answered.

Satisfied there was no immediate threat, the sheriff walked up to Fleet. He raised his chin. "You're in my town and you've got my people in a spell. You'd better start talking, and fast, or there will be hell to pay."

"Did someone say hell?" Shade StormIron appeared in the back of the room, wearing a cheeky smile.

Fleet hadn't seen the reaper since the crash, and he wasn't at all happy to see him now. He moved closer to Infiniti, unsure about the reaper's motives and why he had appeared, since Infiniti was clearly alive. Or was something about to happen to her? He rubbed his fingers together, ready to act if needed.

"Can someone please tell me what's going on?" Infiniti called out.

"Allow me," Shade said, eager to join the group. "Shade StormIron here. Reaper and comedian extraordinaire. Good looking, too." He winked. "Listen, doll. Time's ticking on that soul of yours. No matter what the year, 2012 or 2018, it's all the same to me. This Transhuman here is the bad guy in this scene. He's a member of the Tainted, after all. Fleet by name, Fleet by nature. Right, cupcake?" Shade sneered at Fleet, and Fleet glared in return.

The reaper moved closer to Infiniti. "You crashed, and he saved you, taking work from me, which I don't appreciate. You see, I'm on a tight schedule, doll, as are you." He slapped his hands together, causing them all to jump. "Anyway, here we have Princess and her mother, both witches. Well, one's half hellhound. These guys are wolf shifters. It's like the Count's birthday party in here. Want to know anything else?"

"You're a reaper? Here for me?" Infiniti gulped. Her face transformed from shocked to freaked out, and then to pissed off. She put her hand on her hip and stuck out her right foot. "Well, take a damn number, because I'm not dying anytime soon."

Smiling on the inside, proud of Infiniti and her spunk, Fleet added, "Tiny has a point. Get the fuck out."

The reaper chuckled. "Fine. But I'll be back, doll. Let Princess know I swung by. She'll be sad she missed me." His attention zeroed in on Infiniti. A deadly expression erased his playfulness. "You can't cheat death."

A blast of wind shot through the room as the reaper disappeared. Thick foreboding crowded the air as the reaper's words sunk in. Fleet knew damn well there was no escaping a death sentence.

Joe held Infiniti closer to him. "Don't listen to that asshole."

Sheriff Kasun shook his head. "Enough of all this. Now release my people so we can figure this whole damn thing out."

Fleet thought he could trust the sheriff, but needed reassurance first. "We are in agreement that I'm no threat?"

The sheriff rubbed the back of his neck. "We are. For now."

With a nod, Fleet flicked out a burst of energy, reviving Lyra and Addie.

"What the hell?" Addie said.

Sheriff Kasun quickly defused the situation. "It's okay. Everything is under control. Joe has found our missing person with this Transhuman named Fleet. He says he means us no harm."

Lyra stepped forward. "A Transhuman? In Havenwood Falls? So that's what Addie and I, and the rest of the coven, were feeling." Lyra looked from Addie to the sheriff. "Back in 2012, I wrote in my journal about the energy shift I had detected—a shift I thought was caused by the girl." She approached Fleet with a look of wonder on her face. "But it was caused by you—a member of the Tainted and a henchman of Tavion's. Your presence has caused quite a stir."

"I'd say calling it a stir would be an understatement," Addie added with crossed arms, summing him up. "I've heard of your abilities to travel through space and time. But why would you do that? Now? With this girl?"

"I'd like to know, too," Infiniti said, her head tilted to the side a little, as if taking it all in but unable to figure it out yet.

With the school closed for the holiday break and the heater turned down, cold air had started to fill the room. Fleet watched the supernaturals with keen interest, wondering why the spirit girl had wanted Infiniti to come to this place, and in this time. He also wondered when she'd appear again, because he had no intention of waiting too long.

"Explain," Addie commanded in a voice that vibrated with witchy strength. "Before we declare you an enemy of the town."

Fleet laughed. "I could kill all of you in a second, before you even knew what was happening, but that's not why I'm here."

Sheriff Kasun stepped forward. "Then why are you here?"

"Yeah," Infiniti interjected. "Why *are* we here?"

Fleet had no idea if he could explain, because he didn't completely understand Infiniti's purpose and why the spirit girl had sent them to Havenwood Falls. And where to start? Should he go into the conflict between the Tainted and the Pure? Explain how their war was linked to the survival of the human race? How Tavion sensed Infiniti had a role to play in Dominique's quest for survival? And that a spirit girl had told him to bring the teen to this place and in this time?

He didn't know the supes in the room, but he knew damn well that secret truths were never kept secret. And his dealings with Tavion were none of anyone's damn business. Instead of going into detail, he settled on offering the most basic of answers.

He pointed his chin at Infiniti. "I brought her here from 2012 because she's important for the survival of the human race. There's something here in this time she needs. I just don't know what yet."

"Whoa," Infiniti whispered as she moved closer to Joe. Lyra and Addie shot each other questioning looks. Even the sheriff had no response.

Addie broke the silence. She kept her stare on Fleet, but addressed her mother. "Mom, should we have Elsmed meet us here?"

The elder woman tapped her chin. "Let me check his aura real quick. If he's clear, we can move this conversation to my house."

"Okay," Addie said.

Lyra approached Fleet with caution. "May I?"

"Have at it," Fleet answered, confident he'd pass whatever scan the woman was about to conduct, because he meant the town no harm.

Lyra held her hands up, palms facing Fleet. She kept them like that for a few long seconds, then lowered her arms back to her sides. "His aura is clear enough for us to go to my house and have Elsmed meet us there."

"Elsmed?" Fleet asked.

"Yes, Elsmed," Lyra responded. "He'll be the one to verify your story."

Everything Fleet had said was true, so he didn't mind any verification procedure. Plus, if he wanted the supes to help him, he needed to cooperate.

"Fine."

"I'll let Elsmed know to meet us at my place," Lyra said.

Sheriff Kasun pulled out his phone. "I'll cancel the APB on the girl."

Even Addie started texting. "I'll notify the coven and the Court that we've got everything under control."

Fleet leaned back against the table as he watched everyone take to their tasks, except Infiniti. Standing with Joe, she kept her gaze down. Her brow knitted together in worry. And when Joe said he'd be right back and left her to say something to the sheriff, her expression switched to one of despair.

He sidled over to her. "It's gonna be okay, Tiny."

Her big brown eyes glistened with tears. "How do you know?"

He smiled. "Because I'm here, and I've got your back."

"So you're a bad guy, but you're really a good guy?"

Fleet paused, thinking of all the things he'd done for Tavion, but quickly pushed those terrifying memories aside. He had learned long ago to compartmentalize his feelings, and right now the girl needed him.

"Something like that. And I'm not gonna let anything happen to you. I got you here; I'll get you home."

"What about that reaper?"

Fleet knew reapers never lied when it came to souls they had to reap. So if Infiniti's number was up, then it was up. He just didn't know when or how. But he did know that she didn't need that laid on her.

"Pfft. Reapers don't know shit."

The worry lines on her face relaxed. She let out a breath she had been holding in.

"Thanks, Fleet."

Joe came back to Infiniti and took her hand. Fleet dropped back, letting everyone do their thing. He thought it funny how the sheriff thought he was calling the shots, when in actuality everyone was doing what Lyra and Addie said. He wondered if the sheriff even knew.

With the plan in place to go to Lyra's, Fleet, Joe, and Infiniti climbed into the sheriff's oversized truck. Darkness engulfed the town as they drove. Except for a few traffic lights from the roads and nearby holiday decorated buildings and homes, the only constant color came from the white snow falling down in sheets.

Following Addie and Lyra, they entered a neighborhood with impressive mansions. Weaving through the streets, they came to a smaller home in the back of one of the estates. Once inside, Lyra set fresh logs in the fireplace. She stacked some kindling underneath and lit it with a match. A small, red flame came to life. It spread quickly, and soon the logs crackled with warmth.

Fleet stayed quiet. He studied every inch of the home while Joe comforted Infiniti, saying her mom would be okay, that they shouldn't try to contact her, and that they'd do everything to help her. Not long into their conversation, the doorbell rang.

"That must be Elsmed," Lyra announced.

Fleet tensed. He eyed the front door. Lyra had said Elsmed would verify his story, but he wasn't sure who Elsmed was or how he'd verify anything, though he guessed it would involve mind reading. Expecting a commanding figure to waltz in, he saw a man of at least a hundred years. Tall in stature for someone so elderly, the slow-moving fossil made his way into the room with the aid of a wooden cane.

"Is this everyone?" the man asked Lyra, scanning the faces with frosty blue eyes.

"Yes, it is."

The old man rested his cane against the couch. He breathed in deep, then let out a slow trickle of air. When he did, his ears took on an arrow shape, growing until they poked through his silver hair. The wrinkles lining his face smoothed out. His nose flattened, his long chin dropped until it almost touched his chest, and he grew to a slender but towering size of well over six feet. He huffed, and looked directly at Fleet.

"So, you are the Transhuman, one of the Tainted, villains by any standards. Yet you say you come here in peace to help this young lady." He motioned at Infiniti with long and skinny fingers. "Is that right?"

"That's right."

"Who sent you?"

"A spirit girl named Abigail."

"Interesting," Elsmed whispered. "And you're aware that I'm here to authenticate your story by reading your mind?"

"Pretty much," Fleet answered, wondering if he was making a mistake by letting the old fae probe his mind.

"I'll only look at what I need," Elsmed added with wise eyes. "Nothing more, nothing less."

Fleet raised his chin. "Well then, let's do this."

"Wait!" Infiniti called out. She went to Fleet's side. "Be careful with him, okay?" she said to the fae. "He's sort of like my ride home."

Elsmed tilted his head at her. "Young lady, I am always careful."

"Good." She gave Fleet's arm a reassuring pat, then went back to Joe. "Go ahead," she said to the fae. "Resume."

Elsmed lifted a brow at her before giving Fleet his full attention. "Now," Elsmed instructed in a serious tone, "be still. This will only take a few minutes."

Fleet locked eyes with the fae. He directed his energy to his mind, guarding the pieces he didn't want Elsmed to see, leaving the barest relevant truth available.

I'm here to help Infiniti, sent by a spirit girl named Abigail, and I mean no harm.

Holding the thought, he felt a warm tingle spread across his scalp. Subtle and light, it traveled from temple to temple, swirling around his head.

"Very good," Elsmed whispered, as if signaling completion of his job.

Fleet expected the fae to break his connection, but he didn't. Instead, the fae's eyes narrowed. His nostrils flared. Fleet felt the fae probe deeper, pressing against his barriers in an effort to seek hidden truths.

"*That's none of your damn business,*" Fleet said with his mind.

Elsmed blinked. He stopped the telepathic interrogation. He stepped back. "I suppose you are correct," he conceded. "But I had to try." Elsmed eyed Lyra and Addie. "What the Transhuman says is true. He is no threat whatsoever to the people here."

"Not even from the Collector?" Addie asked.

"The Collector?" Fleet asked.

"A person of interest," the sheriff answered.

"And if you don't know who it is, then it's not your business," Addie added.

Elsmed retrieved his cane. "Correct, not even from the Collector. But I recommend the Transhuman complete his business and move along quickly. His kind always leads to trouble."

"Trust me, I don't want to be here any longer than I have to," Fleet agreed, thinking he needed to hurry and figure out what Infiniti needed to do in this time before Tavion could catch on that something was up. The last thing the peaceful town needed was a madman like Tavion coming for a visit.

Elsmed engaged his glamour, his body morphing back into a regular old man. "I'll let you all get on with it. Reach out to me should you need me again, Lyra."

With the fae gone and the night stretching out, Lyra decided everyone had had enough for the evening.

"Infiniti," Lyra said, "you can stay with me while we sort this whole thing out."

"That's fine with me," the sheriff said, looking tired and worn out. Fleet wondered who the Collector was and what kind of threat he posed to the town. He could sense it was bad, but didn't ask. The last thing he needed was to be pulled into another battle.

"Me, too," Addie said. "My plate is full with other—" She paused, as if finishing the sentence would reveal some sort of secret. "Projects." She turned to her mom. "Unless you need me on this."

Lyra picked up the metal fireplace poker and stirred the fire. "The town is plagued with threats of late. If I can take this piece of worry away from you and the others, then I'm happy to do it. Besides, our time travelers mean us no harm. I'll help them find what they seek, so they can be on their way."

"Yes," Infiniti cut in. "Please. I just want to get home."

Fleet's sentiments echoed Infiniti's, because back in Houston in 2012, Tavion was still hunting Dominique. He needed to accomplish whatever needed to be done, and get back before too long.

"It's settled then," Addie announced. "Infiniti will stay here. And Fleet will stay—"

"I don't need anybody arranging my accommodations."

"Suit yourself, tough guy," Addie said with an eye roll.

Fleet made his way to the door, itching to be alone. "I'll be fine on my own. Be back in the morning."

Outside in the cold, Fleet shoved his hands in his pockets. He started walking to the back of the neighborhood. Finding a dark place surrounded by trees and shrubs, he crouched down. He put his hand on the snowy ground. He thought of transporting to Houston in his proper time so he could check on things, but knew Tavion would detect his presence. So instead, his thoughts went to the Boardman River in Michigan, the place where he used to live before Tavion marked Dominique for death. He loved it there—magnificent trees, the peaceful river, the fresh air. He spent a lot of time there thinking and getting away from things.

Eyeing Lyra's house, he thought Infiniti would be fine with her for the night as he used his energy to go home.

CHAPTER 9

*I*nfiniti felt safe in Lyra's cozy and quaint home, but when Fleet left and Sheriff Kasun and Addie followed, she didn't feel so safe anymore. Feeling a pull toward Joe, and not wanting him to go, she watched him leave, too.

Alone and scared, she wished to be home with her mom. And then she wondered if she'd even make it home. A sinking feeling settled in her gut. She thought of her house, her comfy bed, the giant purple *I* painted on her door, her friends and relatives. A feeling of homesickness the size of Texas settled deep inside her, prompting an aching pain in her heart.

When she left Houston for Colorado, she had high hopes for a great time with her cousins, and possibly even a holiday romance. But when she and her mom got on that plane and they almost crashed, it was as if the bad luck from that event followed her. Staring at her hands, missing Joe's warm and comforting touch, she thought about their almost kiss in the classroom. So far, meeting him was the only good thing to come out of her ordeal.

"Dear," Lyra said, pulling her back to the moment. "Would you like something to eat or drink?"

Her stomach churned with anxiety, but her head still throbbed. "Something to help with my headache would be great. Thank you."

"Altitude getting to you?"

Infiniti rubbed her forehead. "Yeah, a little. I haven't acclimated yet."

"I've got the perfect thing for that," Lyra said with a comforting smile. "Come on."

Infiniti followed Lyra through the living room and to the kitchen. The creamy beige walls and wood floors were perfect for the peaceful Colorado home. She sat at the small round table while Lyra busied herself in the kitchen. She eyed her clothes. She had slipped them on that very morning, in the inn with her mother. For her it had only been hours, but for everyone in Havenwood Falls, six years had passed. She wondered if her mom was okay, and what her life looked like now that Infiniti had been gone for so long.

She was distracted from her somber thoughts when Lyra set a mug in front of her, along with a plate of cookies.

"I've made you a drink with some special herbs that will help your head. The sweets should do you good, too."

"Thank you," Infiniti said. She sipped the floral-smelling water, then helped herself to the food. With each drink of the liquid, she started feeling better. The lingering aches and pains in her body from the car crash began to fade. The clench in her gut released. She even noticed her shoulders relaxing.

Realizing the effect the concoction was having on her, she marveled at her host. "Wow. I don't know what you put in that drink, but I feel so much better."

Lyra chuckled. "I agree, it's good stuff."

Infiniti leaned forward. "Can you show me how to make it?"

"And give away the secret family recipe? I don't think so." Lyra smiled and sat across from her with her own mug in hand. "But I do have an endless supply, should you need another serving."

Together they drank and ate. As the seconds turned into minutes, Infiniti started feeling like her old self. With her worries in manageable mode, and her body relaxed, she asked, "What now?"

Lyra thought for a moment. "How about a good night's sleep? That's what. We can face our worries in the morning." Lyra reached for

Infiniti's hand and squeezed. "Everything will work out. It always does."

Lyra reminded Infiniti of her mother—boldly optimistic despite mounting odds. She liked an outlook like that, and was glad her mother had raised her to believe in the impossible. A feeling of hope grew in her. She smiled and put her hand on top of Lyra's.

"You're right. I'm here for a reason. I can feel it. We're gonna find out what it is, and everything will be okay."

Lyra nodded. "Indeed."

After finding some of Addie's pajamas that were small enough to fit her petite frame, Infiniti took a long hot shower and settled into the queen-sized bed of the first floor guest room. Laying on her back, she stared at the ceiling. With her fear in check, her thoughts drifted to Joe.

"Joseph Greg," she said out loud to herself, liking the way his name sounded. He was the first normal guy to show interest in her. Except, he wasn't exactly normal. Tall, gorgeous, with sparkling hazel eyes and chiseled features, he was perfect . . . for a wolf shifter. Oh, and one not in her same time.

She grabbed her pillow and slammed it over her face, thinking she had the worst luck with guys. She let out a groan when she heard a tapping sound coming from the window. She slid her pillow off her face. She strained her ears. The tapping sounded again, but louder. She sat up, got off the bed, and tiptoed to the window. She placed her shaky fingers on the thick curtains, and paused. She wasn't in Houston suburbia, but supernatural crazy town. Visions of deadly creatures lying in wait on the other side of the glass popped into her mind. But then another thought came to her. What if it was Joe? She grabbed a candlestick from her bedside table to use as a weapon, just in case.

"Please be Joe," she whispered to herself.

She pulled the curtain to the side. She peered into darkness before noticing Joe. He was crouched down, as if keeping out of sight. He smiled when he saw her, and a host of butterflies exploded in her stomach. He pointed to the lock on the window and mouthed the word open.

Placing her weapon on the floor, she moved her hands to the lever. She popped it to the other side, and then pulled the window up. A surge of frigid air swept through the room. She shivered with cold as Joe hurried through the opening and closed the window behind him. He swept clumps of snow off his shoulders.

"Hey," he smiled. "Hope it's okay that I came by to check on you."

She combed her hair back behind her ears, trying to hide her excitement at seeing him. "Yeah, sure. It's great."

A knock sounded on her door. She sucked in her breath. Her eyes grew wide. Joe's eyes darted around the room, looking for a place to hide.

"I don't mind visitors," Lyra called out, "as long as they're announced and seen in the living room."

Infiniti cleared her throat. "Sorry, we were—"

"Going to the living room, right now," Lyra commanded. "And Joe?"

"Uh." He cleared his throat. "Yes, ma'am?"

"If your parents don't know you're here, please tell them."

Joe grinned like a kid caught with his hand in the cookie jar. Infiniti thought he looked so cute like that. "Yes, ma'am."

She stifled her laugh until Lyra's footsteps faded away. "We just got busted."

Joe flashed her a sheepish grin. "Sorry."

She pulled the blanket from her bed and wrapped it around her shoulders. "Come on. Before we get in even more trouble."

They made their way down the hall and to the living room. The logs in the fireplace had reduced to glowing embers. The fading light cast the room in dark shadows, making everything look slightly sinister. Infiniti shivered. Joe must've thought she was cold, because he went to the fireplace right away.

"Here," he said. "Let me stoke up the fire."

He took fresh logs from a stack on the hearth. He placed two chunks of wood on top of the dying ash. He shifted them around with the poker until flames caught in the middle.

"There," he said, sitting next to Infiniti on the couch. "Better?"

The glow of the revived fire and the warmth from Joe calmed her instantly.

"Yes, much better. Thank you."

He pulled out his phone and started texting. "Gotta let my dad know I'm here."

She waited, worried his dad wouldn't let him stay. After a quick exchange, Joe set the phone on the coffee table. "All good. I can stay."

She hid her relief and played it cool, not wanting to show too much excitement about him staying.

"So . . ." she said in a nonchalant tone, searching for the right thing to say.

"So . . ." he repeated.

A nervous laugh escaped her lips. She stared into his dreamy eyes, thinking she could get lost in them.

"Infiniti Clausman," he said with a smile. "From Houston, Texas. I still can't believe you're here. In the flesh. Next to me on this couch." He took on an expression of wonder. "It's crazy."

She angled her body toward him. "I know. Right?" She looked around the room. "This place, this town, the people." She pictured him in wolf form, remembering how he had fallen over onto the snow, his body contorting as he transformed. "I can't believe you're really a wolf shifter."

"Yeah, I really am."

"What other kinds of people live in Havenwood Falls?"

"You mean, what other kinds of supes?"

She pictured a town where all kinds of paranormal people walked around freely. Like Halloween, but every day. "Yeah, supes."

"Well, we've got vampires, ghosts, fae, gargoyles, demons—"

She grabbed his arm and squeezed. "Demons?" A hard shudder moved through her body. "As in, evil spirits that kill people?"

He took her hand. "It's not like that. We live in peace together. We're not killing each other."

"Peace? With a demon? Seems hard to believe."

"We do have some crazy stuff that happens from time to time, but yeah, we pretty much live together in peace." He started playing with her fingers. "There's nothing to be afraid of in this town. I promise."

As they sat close, staring into each other's eyes, the rest of the world seemed to fade away. It was just her, a gorgeous guy, and a romantic fireplace.

"I feel like I've known you forever, even though it's only been a really long day," she said in a low voice.

He took on a serious expression. "It hasn't been a day for me, Infiniti. For me, it's been six years of thinking about you. Six years of wondering who you are and where you went. Six years of longing to see you again." He traced the side of her face with his finger. "It's hard to understand, but for six years you've been in my mind. In my heart. Not once have I stopped thinking about you."

She melted inside. Her heart hammered against her chest. She had never really believed in love at first sight, until meeting Joe.

"Really?"

He stared into her big brown eyes. He brought his hands up to her face. They felt strong and warm against her skin.

"Yes, really."

Like magnets, their bodies moved closer. Their lips parted. Infiniti closed her eyes, ready for her first kiss, when a crashing bang rocked the house. She let out a gasp as Joe jumped to his feet.

Lyra rushed into the room. She flicked on the light. "What was that?"

"I don't know," Joe said. "But it sounded like it came from the front door."

Lyra moved quickly to the front of the house. Infiniti and Joe followed. Shaking like a leaf, wondering what the noise could be, Infiniti envisioned a horrible monster coming for her. Or maybe even that creepy reaper.

Joe placed his hands on the door. He took in a series of small sniffs. "All clear."

Lyra moved her hands around, as if sifting through the air. "Agreed. There's nobody there."

Lyra opened the door. On the ground was an oversized rock with a note tied to it. A huge indention marred the wooden door. Lyra frowned, eyeing the damage.

"Spirits," she whispered.

"Want me to sweep the area?" Joe asked, working his jaw with determination.

"That won't be necessary. But thank you, Joe."

Lyra picked up the rock, stepped back inside, and shut the door behind her. She slipped the parchment out from the brown string. She unfolded the paper. The note read in all caps:

THE GIRL AND THE TRANSHUMAN MUST GO

Infiniti covered her mouth. Her spine tingled with fear. The scrawled print screamed anger and hate. "I'm not safe here," she said between parted fingers.

Fleet appeared behind her. "You are as long as I'm around."

He stomped past her and Lyra and opened the front door. Clumps of snow fell from the sky. A wintry wind whistled in the air. Joe joined him on the porch.

"See anything?" Fleet asked Joe.

Joe narrowed his eyes and scanned the area. "No. You?"

"No."

Back inside, Lyra held the note in her hand. She furrowed her brow. "I need to tell Addie about this. Please excuse me." Before she turned and left the room, she added, "Gentlemen, if you wouldn't mind staying the night, I'd be most appreciative."

"Me, too," Infiniti whispered.

"Yes, ma'am. Of course," Joe said.

"Sure," Fleet added.

Infiniti watched Lyra walk to her room. The expression on the woman's face told her things were bad. She moved up close to Joe and slipped her arm around his.

"I'm so freaked right now."

"It's okay. I'm here with you, and I'm not leaving."

Fleet worked his way around the room, as if securing the place. "Same here, Tiny."

The warning on the note struck fear in her, but having Joe and

Fleet around definitely made her feel better. Resolving her will, she decided her best course of action was to stay near them. Going to sleep in her room, alone, was the last thing she wanted to do. Still clutching the blanket around her shoulders, she eyed the couch and the two oversized cushioned chairs up against the wall.

"I think we should all stay in this room tonight. Together. You know, safety in numbers and all that."

"Good idea," Joe said. "You can take the couch, and Fleet and I can make do on the chairs." He looked at Fleet, who was still moving about the room. "That cool with you?"

"Sure."

Relieved at their plan, Infiniti went back to the guest room to collect the pillows. With her arms full, she remembered the basket she had seen earlier. It was overflowing with blankets. She clutched the pillows in one arm and grabbed a few blankets with the other. Armed with slumber party supplies, it occurred to her that she was about to have a sleepover with two super hot guys. The circumstances could've been a lot better, but she'd take it.

Back in the living room, she saw Fleet standing near one of the windows. Arms crossed and leaning against the wall, he kept a steady lookout. He looked tense and deadly, but in that moment she saw something else in him. Something that resembled loss. Maybe even heartache. She wondered what his story was, and if she'd ever find out.

Joe went over to help with her supplies. Together they tossed everything on the couch. Joe indicated with his thumb at Fleet.

"I don't think he's gonna need any of this stuff."

"Maybe not, but there's plenty for him in case he's interested."

She put a pillow and a blanket on one of the chairs for Fleet, then handed a pillow and a blanket to Joe. She made herself comfortable on the couch, finding the cushions a lot cozier than she imagined. Joe moved his chair closer to her.

"Do you mind if I prop my feet up by yours?"

Her heart fluttered. "I don't mind at all."

He tugged off his boots. Sitting back in his chair, he kicked up his feet by hers. At first, she scooted her feet over, but as they talked about anything and everything into the night, their feet ended up intertwined.

Talking with Joe felt like a dream, as if her brain had imagined the most perfect guy and made him come to life. He loved Cheetos, sci-fi movies, all things chocolate, and amusement parks. He laughed at her jokes and understood her perfectly.

"Tell me about your life back in Houston," he said.

"Well," she said. "It's the regular boring stuff. School, homework, getting ready for graduation, hanging with friends. You know."

Joe didn't say anything for a while. "Does the hanging with friends part include a boyfriend?"

She stopped her foot from rubbing against his, nervous because she had never had a real boyfriend or even kissed a guy before and didn't want to say so.

"No, no boyfriend."

He nudged her foot with his. "Good."

A moment of quiet descended on them. Fleet had long disappeared to another part of the house, and Lyra had been asleep in her room for hours. With the fire out, the only light in the room came from slivers of moonlight through the blinds from the nearly full moon outside. With their feet snuggling against each other, Joe said, "I really like you, Infiniti."

Her heart leapt. A pleasing tingle swirled around in her stomach. They had almost kissed twice, and each time had been interrupted. She thought of getting up from the couch, sitting on his lap, and finally meeting her lips to his. She could almost feel her hands working their way up his neck and her fingers working their way through his hair. Heat filled her body, and suddenly she knew what people meant by needing to take a cold shower.

She drew in a deep breath and told herself to calm down. "I really like you too, Joe."

Somewhere between talking, laughing, and foot flirting, Infiniti fell into a deep and peaceful sleep believing somehow everything would work out.

CHAPTER 10

*J*oe stayed up all night watching Infiniti sleep. He loved the way her mouth slightly parted, the way her long dark hair covered half her face. She made a light snore every other breath, and sometimes her petite nose would twitch. He could look at her for hours and never get tired.

"Does she know?"

Fleet came into the room and sat on the other chair. He leaned over and placed his elbows on his knees. Joe had a feeling he knew what Fleet meant, but asked anyway.

"Know what?"

"That you're called to her."

When wolf shifters were called to someone, it was for life. He had suspected his attachment to her was more than a crush, but didn't know for sure until he saw her at Burger Bar and his heart sang to hers. He hadn't said anything to anyone about it, and wondered how Fleet knew.

Joe slid his feet off the couch. He turned to face Fleet all the way. "No, she doesn't."

"Good," Fleet said. "She doesn't need to know, got it?"

His heart ached, because he knew they could never be a thing. He loved her with everything he had, and no one would ever compare.

Eventually, she'd find whatever she needed in Havenwood Falls and go back to her proper time and place. What good would it do for her to know how he felt?

"Yeah, I got it."

"As soon as we figure out what she needs from this place, we're gone."

"I said, I got it," Joe shot back with intensity.

"Okay, then," Fleet said, getting up and leaving the room.

Joe exhaled. He eyed Infiniti. As much as he didn't like it, Fleet was right. He had to let her go, no matter how much it would suck. And he couldn't let her know how he felt. Not ever.

Somewhere between watching Infiniti and worrying about her, Joe fell into a restless sleep.

THE SAVORY AROMA of bacon tickled Joe's nose. It registered in his brain and traveled all the way to his stomach, waking him with a rumble.

He eyed the couch and saw that Infiniti had already woken up. The room was empty. He got to his feet and stretched, then made his way to the bathroom. He splashed water on his face and toweled it dry. He stared at his reflection in the mirror and said, "You have to let her go."

His head hung low as his directive lingered in the air for a bit before he went to the kitchen. Infiniti and Lyra were working on a spread of scrambled eggs, bacon, and hash browns.

Infiniti lit up when she saw him. "Good morning."

He tried not to sound too excited to see her. "Good morning."

"Sleep okay?" Lyra asked.

"Yes, thanks," he lied, joining them at them stove. "You all need any help?"

"Sure," Lyra said. "If you could pour juice in the glasses, please."

Joe eyed three glasses on the set table. "No Fleet?" he asked.

"No," Lyra said, placing the cooked food on the table. "He's out, trying to make headway on how to get Infiniti home."

His gut twisted at the idea of losing Infiniti, but he pushed it aside as he went to the refrigerator for the juice. He poured the orange liquid into the glasses and sat down. He thought of the note and how Lyra had retired to her room with it in her hand.

"Did you figure anything out about the note?"

Lyra sighed. "No, and I tried all of my tricks. Whoever wrote the note and threw the rock did a good job concealing their identity."

"But I'm not in any danger here," Infiniti chimed in. "Lyra and I already discussed that."

"Correct." Lyra motioned about with her hands. "My home is secure."

They ate for a bit in silence when Joe thought of the Cold Moon Ball. It was in one day, and it was the event of the year. He'd been helping his mom prepare for weeks. As much as he wanted to stay all day with Infiniti, he knew his mom would need him back home to finish preparations.

"Today is Friday," he said out loud.

"Yes, it is," Lyra responded.

"I told my mom I'd help her finish preparing our offering for the Cold Moon Ball." He eyed Infiniti. "The ball is tomorrow."

Infiniti set her fork down. "A ball? Called the Cold Moon Ball? What kind of ball is that?"

Joe always had mixed emotions about the ball. He was never too thrilled about having to get dressed up for it, but he loved all the food and always had a fun time with his friends. "The cold moon is what the full moon is called in December. It's called the cold moon because the weather is so cold."

Lyra wiped her mouth with her napkin. "The ball celebrates the legend of protective spirits that keep the residents of Havenwood Falls from freezing to death during the harsh winter months. It starts at sunset with an elaborate feast in the town community center known as the Annex, then moves to a large ballroom in the Mills mansion."

"Wow, a ball," Infiniti said with wide eyes. "I've never been to a ball."

Suddenly Joe felt as if he and Infiniti were the only ones in the room. Nothing else mattered but spending as much time with her as he could before she had to leave. To hell with playing it safe.

"Do you want to go with me?"

"Wait a minute," Lyra said. "It may not be the wisest thing—"

"Yes!" Infiniti interjected. "I'd love to!"

"Great," Joe said with a grin. He faced Lyra. "My family will be there. So will the whole pack. She'll be safe."

Lyra looked from Joe to Infiniti. Joe could tell she knew how they felt about each other. But would she allow Infiniti to go to the ball?

"If you were still in town," Lyra said to Infiniti, "I was going to stay home with you during the ball." Joe's heart dropped. He could see the matching disappointment on Infiniti's face. "But," Lyra continued, "if you'll still be here, and since you have a date with someone who knows a thing or two about protection, I don't see why you can't go. Some of the Luna Coven and I will be there too to watch over things."

"Oh, thank you!" Infiniti said, beaming with excitement.

The tense mood that had lingered in Joe's gut since his conversation with Fleet changed to an outlook filled with possibility. Leaving Infiniti with Lyra, feeling confident in Infiniti's safety with one of the wisest and most powerful witches in Havenwood Falls, and knowing Fleet would appear if needed, Joe set out for home to help his mother.

Joe told his parents he was taking Infiniti to the ball. Since his dad was a police officer and was there when she crashed in 2012, he already knew all about Infiniti and had filled in his mom, but they had a ton of questions anyway. Joe told them everything, leaving out the part about being called to her, because it didn't matter. One way or another, she'd be leaving Havenwood Falls, and he couldn't change that. But if he could have one amazing night with Infiniti, he was going to take it.

When he finished doing everything he needed to do at home, he hurried back to Lyra's to have dinner with Infiniti and watch a movie. Like a couple who'd been dating forever, they laughed at the same stuff and finished each other's sentences. And before he even realized it, it was almost midnight. He would've stayed all night if he could've, but his dad had ordered him home by the stroke of twelve. He didn't show up again until it was time to pick up Infiniti for the ball.

Dressed in his tuxedo, he waited a few seconds in his car outside the house before going to Lyra's front door. His heart was going bonkers. His hands were a sweaty mess. He wiped them on his pants and gripped his knees.

"Be cool," he said to himself, exhaling one last time before getting out of the car and going to the front door.

He rang the bell. He shifted from side to side. Finally it opened, and there stood Infiniti. She was wearing a purple dress fit for a princess. Long and flowy, it—and she—looked magical. He noticed his mouth was open, and he forced himself to close it.

"Wow. Infiniti, you look beautiful."

She smiled. "Thanks, Joe. You look incredible, too. So handsome."

He held out his hand. "You ready?"

"Yes."

Lyra came up from behind Infiniti. She draped a long black coat around Infiniti's shoulders.

"See you two there," she said.

Joe tried to act cool walking Infiniti to the car, but it was like he couldn't think. He fumbled with the door handle. He dropped the keys. He even sat in his car for a few seconds forgetting how to start it.

Infiniti laughed. "You okay?"

"Yes," he said, pulling it together and finally driving away from the house. "Actually, no. You have an effect on me."

"I do?"

He shifted gears. "You most definitely do."

Infiniti folded and unfolded her hands on her lap. She even started twirling her long hair as if she didn't know what to do with her hands. He smiled to himself, knowing she felt the same way about him.

"So where are we going exactly?" she asked.

"The Cold Moon Ball starts with a dinner at the Annex."

"The Annex?"

"It's an old warehouse complex that's been updated to connect the buildings. Havenwood Falls has a lot of functions there. There'll be tons of food and even some games for those who don't mind braving the elements." He gazed out the window. "And tonight seems like a great night. Cold, but clear. Great for moongazing."

Infiniti peered up at the sky. "Does the full moon, you know, do anything to you?"

"No." He smiled. "My pack's not like that. For us, we're stronger during a full moon, but that's all."

"Oh, I see," she said. A few seconds passed, and Joe could tell she was processing everything. "And after the Annex, then what?"

"We'll be escorted by wagon to the Mills mansion for the dance."

They pulled up to a parking spot. Joe turned off the car and faced her. He lost his words for a second, her beauty nearly taking his breath away. He even thought of going in for that kiss, but thought it wasn't exactly the right moment.

"You ready?"

The whole town had been abuzz about the girl from 2012 who had suddenly reappeared at Burger Bar. Joe knew all eyes would be on them, but he didn't care. All he wanted was to be with her as long as he could. Make every moment he had with her count.

"Yes," she said, looking nervous and excited. "I'm ready."

Staying close and holding hands, they worked their way through the crowd. Joe introduced Infiniti to his parents and his little brother, Boris. A few friends from school even came over for some introductions. He hadn't seen Kase or his family yet, and figured they were running late. But his favorite part of the evening was watching Infiniti ooh and aah over the extravagant holiday decorations.

"It's pretty phenomenal, isn't it?"

She squeezed his hand. "It sure is. Thank you for inviting me."

Bells started chiming, signaling everyone to make their way to the eating area. Joe directed Infiniti to the long tables. Not wanting to be in the middle of the action and having lost sight of his family, he chose a semi-secluded table at the far end of the room. They sat across from each other, and as soon as they did, waiters approached from the sides of the rooms. They draped napkins on their laps, filled their glasses with water and tea, and set down plates piled high with food.

Infiniti's eyes bulged. "This is like Thanksgiving on steroids."

Joe took his fork and knife and started cutting into the turkey. "You could say that."

After the guests had eaten as much as they could, the servers appeared again. This time they whisked away the dinner plates and set down trays of every dessert imaginable.

"I don't think I have enough room in me," Infiniti groaned.

Joe waved his fork around the delights. "There's no room for cookies, pies, cakes, and brownies?"

She laughed. "No, there's not."

Joe set his fork down. He could've devoured the cake, but didn't want to stuff his face too much. At least not while wearing a tuxedo and sitting in front of the most beautiful girl he'd ever seen.

With their settings cleared, Joe found himself leaning over the wooden table to get closer to Infiniti, and she did the same. Entranced with each other like that, they laughed and chatted while the party went on all around them. After a while, they began to notice the quiet in the room. They looked around and found the space practically empty.

"Oops," he said. "We'd better get going so we don't miss the last wagon."

"Sure. But I need to go to the ladies' room first."

Joe walked Infiniti to the restroom. Standing outside and waiting for her, he spotted a young girl on the other side of the room, all alone. She was wearing a long white dress and had long fair hair. She started walking over to hm.

"Hey, are you lost?" he asked when she got near. He crouched down so they could be at eye level. "Where are your parents?"

"You have to help save her," the little girl said.

Joe did a double take. "What?"

"Saving Infiniti is the only thing that matters right now. Understand?"

"The last wagon is leaving in five minutes!" someone called out.

Joe looked in the direction of the voice and gave a wave. When he brought his eyes back to the girl, she was gone. Stunned, he knew she had to have been the spirit Fleet was looking for, the girl he had said was named Abigail. Flustered, he wondered how he could get in touch with Fleet, when Infiniti came out of the bathroom.

"I'm ready," she announced.

Joe rubbed his hands on his pant legs, making a quick decision not to tell her about the girl. He knew it would freak her out.

"Uh, yeah, okay. Let's go."

Glued to her side, and scanning the area around him with every step, he led Infiniti to the area where the last wagon was lined up. He helped her up, and then joined her on the bench. They sat close together, and Joe put his arm around her. The wagon rolled away from the Annex and started its slow-moving trek through the town.

They passed lit and decorated businesses before turning into a neighborhood with lit and decorated mansions. Joe had thought the wagon ride would be the perfect spot for that kiss he'd been longing to give her, but now he was on red alert, eyeing every passerby on the street and investigating every shadowy corner with his heightened vision.

Infiniti put her hand on Joe's knee. "Hey, you okay?"

"Yeah," he said, hiding his worry. "I'm great."

The wagon came to a halt before Infiniti could say anything else. Joe hopped out first and then helped her down. He let Infiniti take in the sight of the exterior of the mansion before ushering her to the door.

"It's like a fairy tale," Infiniti whispered.

Joe watched her marvel at the impressive concrete stairs that led up to the front door of the enormous house. Lights adorned every inch of the façade. Lively symphonic music drifted in the air. He was so used to coming to the Mills mansion, he hadn't really thought of how an out-of-towner would react to seeing it.

"Now *that's* a mansion," she said. She lifted her skirt before taking her first step, then she spotted two large stone statues. She pointed. "Are those dragons?"

"Yes," Joe said, thinking he'd skip the explanation that old man Mills could shift into a frost dragon. Right now he needed to get her into the house and find Fleet. "Those are dragons."

He matched her stride up the stairs, stopping himself from hurrying her along. The last thing he wanted to do was scare her. Besides, he had already decided on his course of action. Get in, make a beeline for the backyard, and figure out a way to summon Fleet.

Once they were inside, an attendant checked Infiniti's coat. A few more steps in, Infiniti held Joe in place.

"Wow," she whispered, admiring the grandeur of the ballroom. "I've never seen anything like this. Look at all those candelabras."

He pushed away his fears over seeing the spirit girl, especially since they were in a safe place surrounded by supes he trusted. "If you think this room is impressive, try looking up at the ceiling."

He watched her gaze roam upward to the sprawling skylight. Crystal clear glass took up every inch of the ceiling. Majestic moonbeams of the cold moon poured through the glass, bathing the space with soft light.

"Incredible," she whispered.

He squeezed her hand, thinking the light of the moon on her dark hair and fair skin made her glow like an angel.

"You're incredible."

She looked up at him, her eyes telling him everything he needed to know about the way she felt for him.

"Do you want to," she half shrugged her shoulders, "dance?"

He wanted nothing more than to get up close to her, to feel her body pressed against his, but his senses were telling him something was up. And it wasn't just the encounter with the spirit girl. He needed to find Fleet right away.

"Why don't we go out to the backyard first? The back patio offers the best view of the moon."

Her eyes widened with delight. "Okay."

He scanned the room, looking for the nearest door to the backyard. He spotted Kase with his family. Not far from them were Lyra and other leaders of the Luna Coven. And then he saw his mom and dad. They were looking at him and Infiniti without really looking. Acknowledging them with a nod, he spotted the double doors he was looking for.

"Come on," he said, taking her hand and making his way outside.

A huge garden sprawled out to the right. To the left was a paved porch with a blazing fire pit in the middle. Everyone must've been inside dancing and eating, because the area was empty. Joe led Infiniti to the fire. Instead of trying to reach Fleet right away, he decided to open up to her. He thought that if something was going to happen, and if she was in danger, he wanted her to know how he felt about her.

Really know.

They sat on the stone seating around the warm blaze. They angled their bodies so that they were facing each other. Their knees touched.

"Infiniti, you—"

She placed her cool and delicate fingers on his lips. "Joseph Greg, I think I might die if you don't kiss me."

Every worry on his mind faded away. There was only him, Infiniti, a warm blaze, a majestic moon, and the calling for her that spread throughout his body like wildfire.

He caressed her face with his hands. He leaned forward. Infiniti parted her perfect lips. She closed her eyes. He was inches from meeting his lips to hers when a rustling in the nearby bushes pricked his senses.

He dropped his hands. He rose to his feet. He issued a silent warning to Infiniti not to make a sound as he moved her behind him. He eyed the darkness that hugged the shrubbery of the garden. His senses analyzed the area—whistling wind, the rustling of leaves, and the menacing padding of animal paws.

Shit, Joe thought to himself, as four wild and hungry-looking wolves emerged from the garden. They were crouched low with teeth bared and saliva dripping. The pack approached with stealth.

"Please tell me they're with you," Infiniti said in a low voice, her words laced with fear.

"They're not."

Joe made a quick assessment of the situation. He needed to shift so he could protect Infiniti, but first he needed to get out of view of the ballroom windows. He couldn't let anyone see him turn into a wolf, especially the humans at the dance. Shifting in public could get him banished, but he was willing to take that risk to protect Infiniti if need be.

"Back up to the shadows," he urged, moving in that direction and increasing the distance between them and the wolves. "When I say now, you get away from me."

"O-k-kay," she whispered, taking Joe's hand in a death grip.

Joe backed out of view of the ballroom with Infiniti pressing up against him. The wolves followed them, matching each step away from the patio. The moonlight highlighted the approaching predators, but then faded as they stepped into the shade of the forest.

Encased in darkness, Joe released Infiniti's hand. "Now!"

Infiniti broke away as Joe's neck cracked. His muscles bulged. His bones broke again and again as his clothes ripped to shreds. He fell to all fours as claws formed. Fangs jutted out of his gums. Fur replaced skin. In full wolf form, he issued a low menacing growl. He crouched down, matching the stance of the predators that were approaching. He readied for their attack, the spirit girl's warning to save Infiniti ringing loud in his head.

CHAPTER 11

*F*leet walked around town in cloaked mode, hoping to trigger something to make Abigail appear. His senses had been tingling since he arrived, and he was starting to have a hard time locking on Infiniti's signature through all the supernatural energy in the air. He needed to find Abigail, and fast. The longer Infiniti was in town, the more at risk she was.

"Come on, where are you?"

He spent a day and a night looking for the young spirit girl. He combed the streets. He searched the woods. Frustrated and angry, he decided to change his tactic. Instead of continuing his search, he thought it'd be best to stay close to Infiniti. If the young girl wanted to show up, she would.

The town had been preparing for a big event, a ball celebrating the cold moon. Peeking in on Infiniti at Lyra's, Fleet saw that she was getting ready. He instantly felt sorry for her. If a reaper was on her tail, then death for her was certain. She'd never be able to be with Joe.

"Poor kid."

Letting her have her time with Joe at the dinner, he made one last sweep of Havenwood Falls before making his way to the mansion where the dance was being held. Almost to the home, his spine tingled with intensity.

"Son of a bitch," he seethed, knowing Infiniti was in danger.

He crouched down. He placed his hand on the ground. He focused on Infiniti's energy signature. He fell into weightlessness. When his boots hit the ground, he found himself on a back porch. A pack of wolves had pounced on Joe in wolf form in the shadowy edge of the forest. They were tearing each other to shreds. Fleet gathered his energy in his hand and threw it at the largest attacking wolf. The bolt slammed into the back of the animal, sending a shriek into the air. Stunned, the beast backed up. The others did, too.

Fleet tossed out another blast. "Get out of here!"

The pack scurried away as the back door swung open. A small group started running toward him. Fleet recognized Joe's parents. Sheriff Kasun followed with a woman in a red dress with long red hair at his side.

Fleet held his hands up to make sure they knew he was helping. "It's okay. They're gone."

Infiniti fell to her knees. She wrapped her arms around Joe's bloodied neck. "They came out of nowhere, and Joe protected me," she said between tears.

"I like to come out of nowhere, too." It was Shade StormIron, appearing before them. He eyed Fleet. "Listen, cupcake, this is twice now you've taken my kill from me. First with this doll whose soul was calling out to me after her crash; and now with this wolf shifter who was moments from certain death. Why do you treat me so badly?"

Fleet fisted his hands at his side. He clenched his teeth. "Their souls aren't calling you anymore, so get out of here."

Shade laughed. "Well, his isn't. But the doll's soul still wants me. I can feel it. I'll be back in due time. Lucky you."

Shade disappeared, but his words lingered deep within Fleet. How could he save Infiniti if that damn reaper sensed her soul was still running out of time? Where was the spirit girl when he needed her?

Joe's mom rushed to Joe's side. Sheriff Kasun and Joe's dad started securing the area so no one inside the mansion knew what was going on outside. The last thing they wanted was a panic at the Cold Moon Ball.

While they bustled about, Fleet ran his fingers through his hair. His body shook with frustration. He'd had it. Pissed and ready to kill something, he hollered, "Show yourself!"

His words echoed all around them. They bounced off the forest trees and nearby mountains. When his voice faded, he saw that everyone was looking at him. He started to offer an apology to the group for his outburst when a hazy white glow came into view. It hovered near them and grew in sharpness and clarity until it formed into the girl.

"I'm Abigail, and I've been waiting for you."

Fleet followed Abigail's line of sight. She was looking at the redheaded woman standing by the sheriff. The woman put her hand on her chest.

"Me?"

"Yes, you," Abigail said. "I didn't know it was you that Infiniti needed until you came into her space. What's your name?"

"I'm Rose. Rose Howe."

Fleet eyed the woman named Rose as she approached Abigail with curiosity. "How can I help you, Abigail?"

Abigail pointed to Infiniti. "We need to save her, so she can help Dominique."

"Who's Dominique?" Rose asked.

"Wait, what?" Infiniti asked, still next to Joe. "Dominique? My friend and neighbor?"

Fleet wanted to interject and explain how Dominique had been hunted by Tavion for lifetimes, but he held his tongue. Abigail needed to explain, because she was the one calling the shots. Besides, the group didn't need all the details.

"Yes, your friend and neighbor. She's important to mankind, and needs to live," Abigail said. "You are vital for her survival, Infiniti. She's going to need you as she faces off against Tavion for the last time."

Stunned, Infiniti had no response.

Fleet thought he should offer some clarification. "Tavion is the leader of the Tainted, and he's been after Dominique for a long time.

81

And if Tavion isn't stopped, he'll kill her and then move on to killing others."

Infiniti stared at Fleet, as if trying to understand. "And I need to help her?"

"Yes," he said. "Apparently, you do."

The lively music from inside trickled to the outside, offering a sharp contrast to their talk of death. Fleet couldn't help but think the world was one messed up place.

"Wow, okay," Rose piped in. "I'm more than happy to help," she said to Abigail, eyeing the group for a second. "What can I do?"

"You need to help Infiniti become a void, so Tavion and his evil forces can't harm her," Abigail said.

Infiniti and Joe moved closer to the conversation. Blood had marred Joe's white coat, and he moved with a heavy limp. He stayed close to Infiniti's legs, pressing up against her.

"Evil forces are trying to get me?" Infiniti asked.

Joe huffed and then growled, signaling his anger at hearing that Infiniti was the target of anything evil.

"Yes, but Miss Rose can help you," Abigail said. "Right, Miss Rose?"

Rose put her hand on her chin. "Are you sure you want me? There are way more powerful witches in Havenwood Falls who can help."

Abigail drifted closer to Rose. She looked up at her with hopeful eyes. "They don't have what you have."

"What I have?" Rose repeated back.

"Yes, what you have."

"What I have," Rose muttered to herself.

"Maybe something at your shop?" the sheriff offered.

Rose squeezed the sheriff's arm. "That's it! The Howe witches date back centuries. I bet there's something in my shop unique to Tavion."

"See? I knew you could help," Abigail said with a smile.

A frosty wind blew through the trees. It swept down onto the back patio, taking Abigail's ghostly form with it like dust in the wind.

Nobody spoke for a while, until Fleet kicked into action mode. "If you can really help Infiniti," he said to Rose, "then we need to get on it, like yesterday."

"Agreed," the sheriff added. "The sooner we help these two accomplish what they're here for, the sooner they can leave."

"Let's do it now then," Rose offered. "Everyone is here at the ball, so there'll be no distractions. Sound good?"

"Sounds good to me," Fleet said.

"Me too," added the sheriff.

"I guess," Infiniti whispered with a faraway look on her face. Fleet could tell she was about to lose it, but he needed everyone to finish with the plan before he could go to her.

"It's settled," Rose announced. "Meet at my shop in one hour. Okay?" She focused on Fleet and Infiniti. "It's called Howe's Herbal Shoppe."

"I know exactly where that is," Fleet said, relieved to finally be getting somewhere with their mission. "Infiniti and I will be there."

Joe's parents left with Joe, so they could patch him up. Sheriff Kasun decided to stay at the party to run interference in case anyone caught on about what was happening at Rose's shop.

For the first time since the crash, Fleet and Infiniti were alone.

Fleet approached the petite teen with caution. Her brows were knitted together. Streaks of blood lined her arms from where she'd been holding Joe. She started shivering and looked like she was in shock. Fleet took off his leather jacket and draped it over her shoulders. She turned into him and started crying against his chest. He patted her back, letting her spill out her tears. Her sobbing slowed down until it finally came to a stop.

"I hate that reaper," she mumbled against his shirt.

Fleet smiled. "So do I, Tiny. So do I." He pulled her away and looked at her tear-streaked face. "Are you okay?"

Infiniti nodded. "I think so."

"Good, because I need you to be strong." He waited for her to answer, hoping she'd have the courage to go on now that they knew what they were there for.

"I'll try."

"Trying is the first step. Now let's get you to Lyra's so you can change and get cleaned up. We've got a witch to meet in an hour."

Infiniti wiped her face with her hands. "Okay."

Letting the revelations of the night slowly sink in for Infiniti, and letting her pull herself together, Fleet waited a few minutes before he summoned his Transhuman skills to transport the two of them to Lyra's place.

Using a key that Lyra had given Infiniti, they went inside. Fleet stayed in the living room while Infiniti fixed herself up. He stared at the clump of ash in the fireplace. He thought about Rose and wondered whether she really had something of Tavion's that could help her fashion a spell. Was it possible that Tavion had somehow exposed himself to one of the Howe witches in the past? He'd spent over a century with Tavion and didn't recall Tavion with a female, let alone a witch, but then again he wasn't glued to Tavion's side either. If Abigail had sensed it, he thought Tavion must've encountered one of them at some point. The dumb bastard.

When Infiniti came back out, she was wearing the same clothes from the crash—dark jeans, a red sweatshirt, and black boots with fur at the top. They were about to go full circle, and Fleet was ready. He was ready to get back to Houston and 2012.

CHAPTER 12

A feeling of weightlessness came over Infiniti. It disappeared when she found herself transported with Fleet from Lyra's house to a sidewalk in a quaint square-shaped shopping area.

"This is it," Fleet said, indicating an antique door with a glass panel in the middle that read *Howe's Herbal Shoppe* in big cursive letters. A shade had been pulled down to prevent seeing inside, but the glass façade to the right of the door showcased a display of soaps, candles, teas, and vials of oil. A dim light shone from the rear of the store, casting a soft glow in the wood-paneled shop filled with wooden shelves.

"You ready?" Fleet asked.

Infiniti thought of Abigail's words, that she needed to become a void so she could help her friend, Dominique. The idea of being caught up in some sort of good versus evil struggle terrified her, because she believed in evil, really and truly believed in it. Even though she had always put up a good front when it came to seeing scary movies with her friends, oftentimes the images on the big screen would plague her for nights. Goose bumps lined her skin. She looked up at Fleet.

"Why me?

Fleet shoved his hands in his pockets. "I ask myself that question all the damn time."

"You do?"

"Yeah, I do."

"And what's the answer?"

Fleet thought of everything he'd been through, and imagined what was still to come. "Because I can take it." He flashed Infiniti an encouraging look. "And you can, too."

She let his words work their way through her. She wanted to match his strength and determination, no matter how freaked she was.

"Damn straight, I can take it."

"Now let's try this one more time." He put his hand on her shoulder. "Are you ready?"

She drew in a deep breath. "I'm ready."

Fleet tapped on the door. It swung open right away, revealing a battered Joe. Stitches lined his forehead and cheeks. One of his eyes was swollen and bruised. A crutch was under his right arm.

Infiniti gasped. "Oh my God, Joe."

She knew his injuries were bad, but couldn't really tell before, with all the fur. Now that he was in human form, she could see all the damage.

"It's okay," he said, ushering them in with a limp. "It looks a whole lot worse than it feels. Really."

"Man, sorry, Joe," Fleet said. "I got there as soon as I could."

"I know, and I'm glad you did. You saved my ass."

"What was up with those wolves anyway?" Fleet asked with a furrowed brow. "Why did they come out and attack like that?"

Joe shook his head. "I don't know. They looked on the hungry side, but my dad thinks someone may have spelled them or something, to get them to come out like that." Joe shrugged. "Maybe the same person who wrote that note and threw it at Lyra's."

"Son of a bitch," Fleet whispered under his breath. He eyed Infiniti. "Guess it's a good thing we're leaving, then."

Guilt at what happened to Joe gripped her. "I guess."

Fleet looked around. "Where's Rose?"

Joe pointed behind him. "Back room."

Fleet went to the back, leaving Infiniti alone with Joe.

Infiniti's lip quivered as she eyed the injuries on Joe's handsome face. She lighted her fingers on his cheek and stared up into his striking hazel eyes. "This is all my fault," she said, her throat clogging over with tears. "You could've been killed because of me."

He took her hand and moved it to his lips. He kissed her fingers. "None of this is your fault. And I'd do anything for you, Infiniti. Anything. Including risk my life."

Standing there with Joe, with the moonlight trickling through the window, she thought him the most amazing person she'd ever met—beautiful in every sense of the word. Everything about him filled her heart, and if soul mates existed, she knew hers was meant for his. But destiny was cruel, and soon she'd be going back to her proper time, with every memory of Havenwood Falls erased.

"I don't want to lose you," she whispered.

He sighed. "I don't want to lose you either."

Moving closer, Joe finally brought his mouth to hers. His lips were soft and smooth, his tongue was velvety, and his breath mixed with hers sent her head into the clouds. He dropped his crutch and held her tight as their mouths connected over and over and over, neither of them wanting to break apart from the other, knowing their first kiss was going to be their last.

Their lips slowly separated, yet they stayed close together, catching their breath.

Joe gazed at her with passion-filled eyes. "I don't know how, and I don't know when, but I'm going to find you, Infiniti Clausman."

Infiniti brushed her lips against his. "You promise?"

He kissed her again, nice and slow. "I promise."

They parted as Fleet came into the room. If he noticed their moment, he gave no indication. "It's time."

Infiniti handed Joe his crutch, and together they went to the back room of the herbal shop. If the smell of herbs permeated the front area of the store, then it was crazy powerful in the back, and with good reason. The walls were lined with wood shelves filled with jars upon jars of twigs, roots, leaves, and powders.

"Wow," Infiniti said. "An earthy candy shop."

Rose was still wearing her long red ball gown. She smiled at her collection with pride. "Impressive, isn't it? I call this back room my office. I keep the popular herbs in the front of the store—sage, rosemary, and vanilla. You know, common stuff. Back here is where I keep the hard-to-find resources. Only supes would know to ask for these products."

Infiniti got up close to the shelves and read some of the labeled jars. "Brahmi, lobelia, woad, and horehound?" Infiniti snickered. "What does horehound do?"

Rose laughed. "Horehound is used for treating respiratory infections. And by the way, none of these are named by me."

Infiniti continued studying the room. A brown antique desk sat in the middle of the space. Books crammed the shelves behind. Some looked modern and new, while others appeared worn and ancient.

"This is so amazing," Infiniti said, marveling at everything around her.

"It is indeed, and this," Rose held up a small leather book, "has the perfect spell for you. These words, combined with the ingredients I've already gathered and mixed, will accomplish what we're after."

Infiniti gulped. She squeezed Joe's hand. "It will?"

"It sure will."

"And the ingredients include something of Tavion's?" Fleet asked, his words laced with disbelief.

Rose nodded. "I cannot share what I have, or how it was acquired, but yes, I have something of Tavion's. The Howe witches have gathered a wide variety of objects and materials over the centuries, especially items belonging to the powerful. As the spirit child suggested, my Howe collection contained something of Tavion's. I had actually all but forgotten I had the item. You may check my potion if you'd like." Rose set her book on the desk. She lifted a small bowl filled with a dark liquid. She held it before Fleet. "Here you go, but please don't touch the contents."

Fleet took the bowl with one hand. He placed his other hand over the top, hovering his palm inches from the rim. He closed his eyes. He face took on a look of concentration as a glowing light shone from his palm. The radiance saturated the bowl, bathing it with his stream of energy. He powered down and handed the bowl back to Rose.

"Tavion's essence is in there, all right," Fleet said. "I'd know it anywhere."

Infiniti found herself pressing against Joe, squeezing his hand in a tight grip. She envisioned all kinds of things of Tavion's that could be in that bowl—blood, hair, pieces of skin. Joe put his arm around her, letting her know everything would be okay.

Rose moved the small bowl to one hand. She picked up her book with the other and tucked it under her arm. She eyed Fleet.

"This Tavion has quite the complicated emotions."

Fleet rubbed his face. "You could say that."

"Well, now that we've got that all established," Infiniti said nervously, ready to finish what they had started before she chickened out, "now what?"

"Now we step into my treatment room."

Infiniti didn't like the sound of that, but followed Rose anyway. The red-haired woman led the group through a door that Infiniti had assumed went to a closet or bathroom. Instead, it connected to a small room like the ones used for massages. There was a long exam table, a small table for supplies, and a chair.

Rose patted the table. "Have a seat right here, Infiniti, and I'll explain the procedure. Everyone else, file in."

Trying not to show any fear, Infiniti got up on the table. Joe stood by her side, still holding her hand. Fleet closed the door and leaned against it.

"While you all were getting here, I came right on over and started researching." Rose flipped through the pages of the book, found her spot, and tapped the page. "This spell prevents harmful energy, either natural or manmade, from reaching you."

"Reaching me?"

Rose set the book down. "You can't prevent someone from trying to harm you, but you can prevent whatever they are sending from reaching you. This spell will do exactly that by creating a sphere-shaped invisible shield around your person."

"Come again?" Infiniti said, confused by it all.

Rose tapped her temple. "Think about it this way. Let's say someone wants to cast a spell that makes you sick. If you are inside a protective shield, like a telephone booth for example, the spell will bounce off. It won't reach you."

Infiniti thought of the TV show with the guy that went into the telephone booth and transported through time. She imagined herself standing inside one of those and someone blasting a laser of death at her that bounced off the glass.

"Nothing can get me while I'm in the booth."

"That's right," Rose nodded. "After you drink my potion, the spell will be specific to Tavion and anyone associated with him."

Infiniti shuddered. She was pretty sure she'd need to drink the goo, but actually hearing Rose say it made her stomach turn.

"This will work against Tavion's cronies, too?" Fleet asked.

"Correct. This spell should be effective against anyone following Tavion's directive," Rose explained.

"So this Tavion guy and his people can't hurt her?" Joe asked. "After you're finished?"

"That's right."

Fleet rubbed his chin. "How long will it last?"

"That part I'm not sure of," Rose admitted. "But hopefully indefinitely."

"What about the spell around the town that makes people forget this place when they leave?" Joe asked. "Can you do something about that?"

Infiniti gripped Joe's hand and pulled it close, hoping for a way to return to this place and in this time. But Rose's face told her there was no way.

"The spell is only effective against Tavion and his harmful influence. Besides, the wards are designed to help, not hurt. So like all people who leave, Infiniti won't remember us or any of her time here." Rose placed her hand on Infiniti's shoulder. "I'm sorry."

"It's for the best, Tiny," Fleet said.

"It really is, my dear," Rose added.

Speechless, Infiniti couldn't say anything. All she could do was hold on to Joe's promise that somehow he would find her, though deep down she knew it was impossible.

Rose got to work. She handed Infiniti the bowl filled with the dark liquid. Infiniti warily eyed the thick substance.

"Is this gonna taste disgusting?"

"Probably," Rose answered, lighting a white candle.

"Great," Infiniti muttered. She held her breath and closed her eyes, pretending she was at a party about to take a shot. She put the glass to her lips and chugged the grossness with one swig. She shuddered. "God, that was awful."

With the goo traveling down her throat, Infiniti watched Rose light an incense candle. She waved it around Infiniti. Burning smoke trailed the air while a heavy woodsy aroma wafted about her.

"I actually love incense," Infiniti said, thinking of her sticks of incense back home.

"Ah, you're a young lady of nature?" Rose set the burning stick on a wooden holder, then took the bowl and set it aside.

"A little," Infiniti said, feeling peaceful and relaxed, thinking Rose had slipped some sort of calming element to the drink. She wondered if it shared some of the same ingredients as the drink she had at Lyra's. Or maybe the calmness came from the pleasing smell of the incense. She wasn't sure, but she was glad for the soothing effect.

Rose rubbed her palms together. "Infiniti, close your eyes. Visualize a circle forming around you, in front of you, and moving all around you completely. And then, above you, behind, and all around you. Essentially, you are enclosing yourself in a sphere. The sphere is permeable. Good energy can come in and bad energy stays out. Especially energy from the Tainted leader known as Tavion and those aligned with him."

Infiniti closed her eyes. Staying with Rose's analogy, she pictured herself standing in an all-glass telephone booth. She immediately felt safe inside, as if nothing could harm her within the enclosure.

"Do you see it?" Rose asked.

"Yes, I see it."

"Are you safe?"

Infiniti felt as if a warm sun was shining on her. "Yes, actually. I feel very safe. Kind of peaceful, even."

"Good, now keep your eyes closed and hold the image while I cast the spell."

Infiniti tightened her eyes. Rose began speaking in a language she couldn't understand. Flowy and almost musical, the words floated around in her head like an ancient rhyme. Believing in their power, Infiniti also started believing in something else—her love for Joseph Greg.

"Okay," Rose announced, pulling Infiniti out of her trance-like state. "It's done."

Infiniti opened her eyes. She looked at Rose. "That's it? I'm protected now?"

"You are."

A quiet hush fell on the group. Fleet broke the silence. "Sorry to say this, but it's time for us to leave, Tiny. Mission accomplished."

Infiniti gulped. "Right now?" For some reason, Infiniti thought she'd have more time for goodbyes, more time with Joe.

"Yes, now."

"I have to agree," Rose chimed in. "You two are not naturally from this time or place. The sooner you can get back to where you belong, the better."

Infiniti exchanged a lovesick look with Joe. "Can I have a minute with Joe?"

"Sure," Rose said. "Fleet and I will wait for you in my office."

Alone with Joe, and still sitting on the table, she pulled him close. She wrapped her arms around his neck, and he kissed her sweetly. They kissed with love, with heartache, and with sorrow, holding on to each other with desperation before they slowly parted. Joe nestled his face in the crook of her neck.

"Please find me, Joseph Greg," she whispered. "Please."

He pulled away and studied her. He traced the side of her face with his fingers. "I will."

He looked down for a second, and then looked back at her, as if struggling to find the right words for something he desperately wanted to say. Infiniti's mind took her to that moment on the mountain when they first met, when she had asked him to say he loved her.

"Joe, tell me—"

"I love you—" he said. "Really and truly, with everything I am, I love you."

She pulled him in and kissed him again, thinking she could kiss him forever, telling him she loved him back. Slowly and reluctantly, they finally separated.

She and Joe joined Rose and Fleet in the other room. Fleet put his hand on Infiniti's shoulder.

"You ready to go back to 2012, Tiny?"

She hesitated with her answer, suddenly consumed with ideas of time travel and alternate time lines. "Will I be the same when I go back? Like my life and my family and my friends? Or will everything be . . . bizarro world?"

"There'll be no bizarro world," Fleet explained. "Time travel doesn't have to be wholly disruptive. What has happened here is a splintering of events. We'll go back to our original timeline, and what has happened here in Havenwood Falls will remain intact in its own timeline."

"Oh, okay," she whispered, confused by it all but trusting Fleet.

Although she was ready to see her mom, she was not at all ready to lose Joe forever. Plus, there was the whole whatever was going to happen to Dominique thing. There were so many scary unknowns in her future, but she refused to let fear or doubt rule her. Like Fleet said, she could take it. And somehow or another, she believed in her heart of hearts that everything would work out and Joe would find her.

"I guess I'm ready."

She and Fleet backed away from Joe and Rose. Wispy gray tendrils oozed out of Fleet's hand. The mist wrapped around her arm, spilling down her body until it formed a small churning circle of vapor beneath their feet.

She kept her eyes on Joe until he slipped out of view and was replaced by the windshield of her rental car. She slammed on the brakes. She screeched to a stop on the side of the road. She looked all around and found herself alone. The radio blared. The smell of Flamin' Hot Cheetos hung in the air. She stepped outside the car and into the cold air. She spun around searching the space around her.

"Fleet?"

She waited for him to appear with his deadly good looks and bad attitude, but he didn't. She was alone. Her thoughts turned to Joe. She wasn't sure when the magic of Havenwood Falls would kick in and erase her memories, but she figured it'd be right away.

Frantic determination seized her. "Joseph Greg, Joseph Greg, Joseph Greg," she repeated as she hopped back in the car and snatched her phone. She opened her text to send herself a message, but was so flustered she dropped the phone. "Dammit."

She scooped it back up, and it rang in her hand, giving her a small heart attack. She looked to see who it was and answered right away.

"Mom!"

"Fin, are you okay? You've been gone a while."

"Oh, Mom! It's you!"

"Of course it's me. Is everything all right?"

"Uh . . ." Her brain scrambled with what to say. "I started driving around to check out the area and lost track of time. I'm so sorry. I didn't mean to worry you."

"It's okay. Just get back soon. I'm starving."

"I will."

She ended the call, then opened up her messages and went back to her text. She stared at the device, searching for the name she had been repeating right before her mother called. Her hand moved to her lips. Suddenly she remembered the tingling from Joe's kiss.

"Joseph!" She typed, *Joseph Greg*. She stopped, her fingers lingering over her phone while she racked her brain for the name of the town.

"Havershire," she said out loud, but thought it didn't sound right.

"Nope, that's not it. Havenshire." She slapped her hands against the steering wheel, knowing that was wrong, too. "Maybe it's not with an H. Maybe it's with a W. Woodenshire, Woodhaven."

She grunted with frustration, when a horn honked behind her. A car pulled up next to hers and stopped. It was an elderly couple. They had their window rolled down. Infiniti rolled hers down, too.

"You need some help?" the lady asked.

Infiniti raised her phone. "No, I'm okay. I was just taking a call. Thanks, though."

"Smart girl," the lady said. "This pass is known for people driving off the cliff."

Infiniti smiled and waved. "Oh, got it. Yeah, I'll be careful."

She rolled up her window as the couple drove off. She stared at the side of the road that edged up to a sharp drop. She shuddered, thinking a plunge off the side of a mountain would totally suck.

And then she realized her phone was in her hand. She looked at it. She noticed an open text to herself with the name Joseph Greg. Nothing more.

"Huh," she mumbled. "Who's Joseph Greg?"

She watched the letters of the name disappear as she pressed the back button. She eyed the blank screen for a second, feeling as if she was forgetting something. She brushed it off, then set her phone in the cup holder. She fiddled with her radio, found a good song, and headed back to her mom and the inn, hoping they could somehow make it to Breckenridge for Christmas.

EPILOGUE

*J*oe stared at Infiniti. He studied every detail, desperate to imbed her image in his brain before she vanished, because he didn't know if he'd really be able to find her once she left Havenwood Falls. Long dark hair, ivory skin, the most beautiful face he'd ever seen. A gray mist oozed out of Fleet's hands. It spilled down to the ground and formed a swirling vapor around their feet. Infiniti's lips parted, as if she wanted to say something, before she plunged from view.

"Infiniti!"

He dashed to the spot where Infiniti had stood with Fleet. He glanced around, as if she'd reappear, but she didn't.

Heartbreaking silence filled the room.

"I'm very sorry, Joe," Ms. Howe said in a low voice.

His heart crumbled. A lump the size of a football lodged in his throat. He felt as if a piece of him had been ripped away, and he didn't know if he'd ever get it back.

"I'll let you have a minute," Ms. Howe added, leaving the room.

Joe couldn't remember the last time he had cried, but seeing Infiniti disappear brought tears to his eyes. He rubbed them away with the back of his hands, forcing himself not to lose it. Not here, anyway.

He put his crutch under his arm and hobbled out of Ms. Howe's office and to the front of the herbal shop. He kept his gaze down, not wanting to make eye contact.

"Thanks for everything, Ms. Howe."

"Sure thing, Joe."

He fumbled with the keys in his pocket as he painstakingly made it out of the shop and into his car. He sat there for a minute, thinking how hours earlier Infiniti was sitting next to him, dressed like a princess for the ball, and now she was gone. He leaned his head against the headrest, thinking of their amazing kiss and the promise he had made to find her.

Could he really do it?

He started his car and headed home. He was driving through the quiet streets of the town when a memory exploded in his brain. A few months after Infiniti had vanished back in 2012, he had a series of dreams of horrible things happening to her, incidents that all resulted in her death. Another car accident, being swept away by a tornado, drowning in the ocean, even catching on fire. He shuddered as the feeling of horror mixed with intense loss worked his way through him.

He thought of that damn reaper and his words.

"But the doll's soul still wants me. I can feel it. I'll be back in due time."

Had they sent her back only to die?

Had they made a horrible mistake?

Joe screeched to a halt. He made a U-turn in the middle of the street and hauled himself back to the herbal shop. Rose was emerging from the front door. He hopped out of his car and rushed over to her.

"It didn't work!"

She huddled into her coat and wrapped her arms around herself. "What do you mean?"

"We sent her back to 2012, and she's going to die there. I know it."

Rose looked away for a second, as if contemplating the possibility. "Listen, Joe. I don't know if you're right or wrong, but I do know a thing or two about destiny, and I can tell you that destiny cannot be changed. Ever." She stared up at the sky. "It's like telling the moon not to be bright. It simply can't be done."

He looked down at the sidewalk, racking his brain for a response, because there was no way he was going to give up on Infiniti. Finally, an idea came to him.

"Okay, fine, I get that about destiny, I really do. But what if her coming here was another type of destiny? A way for the right destiny to counter the wrong destiny?" He stopped, thinking his words weren't making any sense and sounded a little crazy, but he went on anyway. "I mean, we didn't bring her here, yet she showed up needing our help. Maybe, just maybe, she needs our help again."

He hobbled forward, waiting for the red-haired witch to give him some sign of hope.

She nodded with a pensive look on her face. "Maybe she does, Joe. But let's get through the holidays first, okay? And we can take up this conversation later."

"Okay, yeah," Joe said. "I'll come by after the new year."

Her offer to help was encouraging, but he couldn't wait until after the holiday break to do something about finding Infiniti. Back home and in his room, he texted Kase, knowing he'd be up at midnight.

Me: Dude.

Kase: Yeah.

Me: Need your help.

Kase: About the girl? Did it work? My dad told me.

Joe wasn't surprised that Sheriff Ric had said something to Kase. And he didn't mind. Kase was his best friend.

Me: Yeah. She's gone.

Kase: Sorry.

Me: It's ok. But I have an idea. Come over tomorrow. I'll fill you in.

Kase: Is it a crazy idea?

Me: Maybe.

Kase: Cool, I'm down. See you then.

Joe set his phone on his bedside table and lay on his bed, exhausted and feeling like crap. But more than anything, he was determined to find Infiniti Clausman. And no one could stop him.

Thank you for reading!
Infiniti & Joe's story continues in
Finding Infiniti.

WE HOPE you enjoyed this story in the Havenwood Falls High series of novellas featuring a variety of supernatural creatures. The series is a collaborative effort by multiple authors.

Havenwood Falls books by Rose Garcia about Infiniti & Joe:

Saving Infiniti
Finding Infiniti
Sun & Moon Academy Book One: Fall Semester
Sun & Moon Academy Book Two: Spring Semester

OTHER BOOKS you might enjoy in the Young Adult Havenwood Falls High series:

Written in the Stars by Kallie Ross
Somewhere Within by Amy Hale
Fata Morgana by E.J. Fechenda
Cast in Moonlight by Ali Winters

Stay up to date at www.HavenwoodFalls.com

ROSE GARCIA

ABOUT THE AUTHOR

Rose Garcia is the author of the critically acclaimed Final Life Series. The saga features gut-wrenching emotional turmoil and heart-stopping action with a diverse and dynamic cast. A lawyer turned writer, Rose has always been intrigued by science fiction and fantasy. More recently, she's been intrigued by a blend of science fiction and reality and the idea that some supernatural events are, indeed, very real. Just ask her about the ghost she used to share a house with. Rose lives in Houston with her husband, two kids, and two dogs. Luckily, there are no ghosts in her current home. For information on Rose's new releases and appearances, sign up for her newsletter at www.RoseGarciaBooks.com/newsletter. You can learn more about Rose at www.rosegarciabooks.com.

ACKNOWLEDGMENTS

I have so many incredible people to thank for helping me bring *Saving Infiniti* to life! First and foremost, I want to thank the amazing Kristie Cook. A visionary like no other, Kristie Cook is the creator and publisher of Havenwood Falls. When I first heard of her project way back when, I knew right away that I wanted to be a part of it. And when I pitched the idea of bringing Infiniti and Fleet from The Final Life Series into the world, she was on board!

To all the Havenwood Falls authors who helped me breathe life into my story: Kallie Ross who shared many of her characters with me including Joseph Greg and his family, Sheriff Ric and Kase of the Kasun pack, and Rose Howe; Justine Winter who let me set her cheeky reaper Shade StormIron on Infiniti's heels; Kristie Cook who let me use the wise and caring Lyra Beaumont and Lyra's daughter Addie; E.J. Fechenda who let me use her mind-probing fae Elsmed; and Tish Thawer who educated me on all things witchy. A special thanks to Regina Wamba for my amazing cover and Liz Ferry for her eagle eye editing! And really, the entire Havenwood Falls author family has been beyond helpful, and I'm so glad to have them in my life!

To my amazing beta readers and critique partners who've been a part of my writing journey for many years: Heather Elliot, Jessica Ramirez, and Wade Moriarty, and my teen readers Olivia and Jake. You guys ROCK! I seriously don't know what I'd do without y'all! And, of course, to the PR professionals who've helped me so much: Amber Garcia and Marya Heidel. Also, a special thanks to my PA Kellie Kortright who helps me so much with my FB fan page! For those wondering where *Saving Infiniti* fits in The Final Life Series, it's an expansion of a scene in *Final Life*, book one in the series. *Finding Infiniti*, due out summer of 2019, will fit into the series after *First Life*, book four in the series.

AN EXCERPT

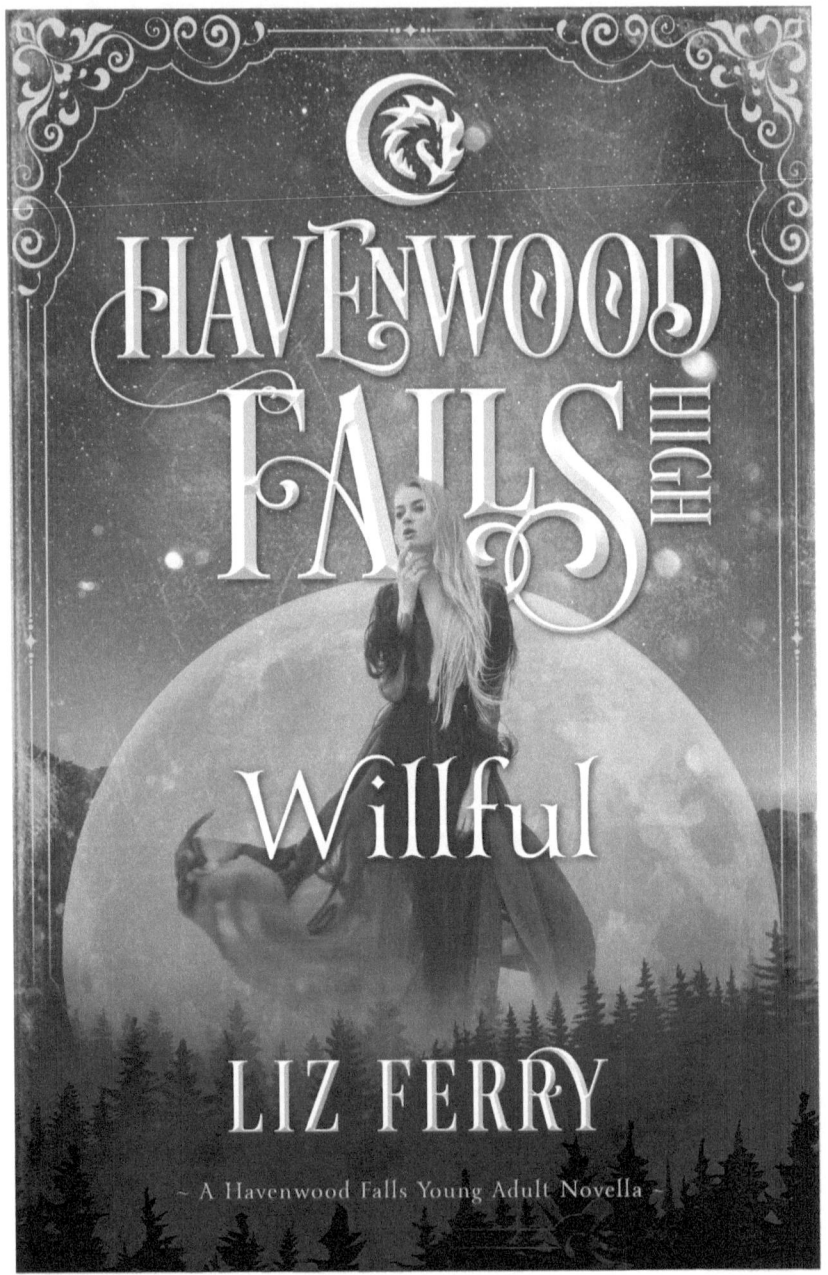

Willful (A Havenwood Falls High Novella) by Liz Ferry

Celeste is used to getting her way—it comes naturally. Now that she's coming of age, she's about to learn why things turn out in her favor so often, and find out some hidden truths about her own identity. She'd better learn fast how to keep her nature under control, before it gets her kicked out of town—or worse.

Jonathan has been on the run for as long as he can remember. Everything he's been taught was in service of keeping his family's secret safe. And this isn't just any family secret—if it gets out, it could mean the destruction of his people. He and his mom hope Havenwood Falls will be a safe haven for them and the secret they protect. But they may have run right into the hands of their enemies.

When Celeste sets her sights on Jonathan, she may be in for her biggest challenge yet. He can't afford a distraction like dating. But every time their paths cross, they're drawn closer together. Let the battle of wills begin.

WILLFUL

BY LIZ FERRY

JONATHAN

It was a bright, sunny day when it happened. If it had been rainy, we would have stayed home, and they would have caught us. But it was cool and crisp, and Mom wanted to take a stroll down to the open-air market to pick up some fresh vegetables. She usually went with Mrs. Viegas, our neighbor, a nice old lady who'd lived in the small mountain town for her whole life, but today she asked me to walk with her, and I did, because I was bored.

We walked along the cobblestone streets, Mom drilling me on history facts, dodging kids playing and women sweeping their stoops. At the market, surrounded by the earthy smells of farm-fresh produce, we picked up tomatoes and cucumbers, onions and potatoes, celery and cabbage. At every booth, Mom stopped to chat with the farmers, asking about their children, their harvest, and their health.

On our way back from the market with a bag full of vegetables, we ran into Mrs. Viegas hurrying down the road. She stopped us with waving arms, but lowered voice. She spoke into my mother's ear for a minute, and I watched my mom's expression turn to panic, matching the old lady's, as her hand came up to clutch the gold pendant she wore. My mother started nodding rapidly, then shoved the bag of vegetables into our neighbor's arms and grabbed my hand.

"*Obrigada, obrigada*," my mother thanked Mrs. Viegas, then turned and ran, dragging me along with her.

I was surprised at the speed with which we were able to leave town. Apparently, Mom had set up contingency plans for getting us out if— when—we needed to run. We ran to Mr. Mata's garage, where my mother pulled him out from under a car and told him she needed her keys. He ran to the office and handed over a set of keys, then pointed to the back door of the shop. Within minutes, we were out of town and speeding down the road to Lisbon.

About half an hour after we left, I looked out the back window to see a thin plume of black smoke rising into the sky above the town that had been our home for the last three years. I hoped Mrs. Viegas was okay.

~

CELESTE

"Celeste! Finally," Margaret said as she opened the door. Her mass of black curls was held back with a thin pink headband, which matched her chiffon dress.

"That's what you're wearing?" I bypassed polite greetings and got straight to the point. "No, no, no. Come on, we still have time," I continued, marching through the front door and up the stairs to Margaret's room, with my friend trailing along behind me.

"What's wrong with it?" asked Margaret. I could tell she was already resigned to the fact that her pale pink party dress from Dress Perfect would be spending the night back on its hanger.

"Well, first, you wore it to Christine's birthday party six months ago. And second, it's . . ." I trailed off, looking the dress up and down, trying to find a way to tell her it would send her crush entirely the wrong message. Catching Margaret's disappointed expression, I softened my tone. "It's just not flirty enough. Tonight's not just the

Sweetheart Dance, it's your first date with Xavier. You've got to show off those curves! Remind him how lucky he is that he landed a date with you."

"Oh . . . yeah, I guess you're right," Margaret conceded, looking to her closet worriedly and adjusting her glasses. "But what will I—"

"Where's that little black dress we got at Callie's?" I interrupted, impatiently flipping through the hangers in the closet.

"Behind the door, but—"

"But what?" I asked, turning to pull the dress, still wrapped in its plastic cover, off the back of the closet door.

"It's so . . . short," Margaret admitted, her eyes glued to the hemline.

I looked at my friend and closed the mirrored closet door in front of her. "Margie," I leveled in my best no-nonsense voice. "Look at those legs. Hike up that long-ass skirt you're wearing and look."

Margaret obliged, shrugging.

"You've got gorgeous gams, girl! You can't not show those things off."

"Gams?" Margaret laughed. "Who says that?"

I giggled. "I couldn't resist. Look at this fantastic flapper dress! I'd be dying to wear this! It's perfect for tonight."

Margaret held up the vintage twenties gown, complete with black fringe and crystal beading. It really was beautiful, and Callie had sworn it was authentic.

"Okay," Margaret caved. "Find me some shoes."

Suppressing a squeal of glee, I dove back into the closet in search of footwear while Margaret changed, and came up with a pair of strappy black heels that were hidden under a mountain of flats. I helped pin her curls into a stylish twist on top of her head, watching her transform from awkward teen to sophisticated young woman before my eyes.

"Perfect!" I exclaimed when Margaret stepped into the shoes and twirled, the fringe floating around her. "Xavier's going to melt, you're so hot."

"Speaking of hot," Margaret said, grabbing her extra-long coat, "I'll need this so I don't turn to ice—and to make it past my dad."

We laughed our way back down the stairs arm in arm, Margaret's shoulders loosening with every step, then freezing when the doorbell rang.

"It's him," Margaret said.

We made it through the obligatory stern looks from Margaret's dad and piled into Xavier's car. Even though it wasn't far to the Annex (nothing was really *far* in our little town), it was too icy to walk more than a block or two in heels.

By the time we got to the Annex, my mood had turned from giddy to glum. I walked into the building wondering why I was even there. With no sweetheart to bring to the Sweetheart Dance, why bother? As I watched Xavier's eyes nearly bug out of his head when Margaret slipped out of her coat, though, I remembered, and I couldn't keep a smile from my lips. My friend had been pining after the object of her desire for months, and I was happy to finally see them on the right track.

Handing my own coat over at the coat check table, I smoothed my hands over my silver sheath dress and looked around. Now that the important part was over with, I'd have to make the best of the evening.

The space inside the Annex had been rearranged to accommodate the event, and I had to admit the decorating committee had done a great job. The stage at the far end was set up for one of the better local bands, the Mountain Monsters, but just now the DJ, on a separate dais to the right, was playing upbeat music and taking requests for slow dances later on.

I turned to my left and headed for the refreshments table. As I turned back with a plastic cup of pink punch, someone walking in the door caught my eye. Someone new.

I watched as he stopped short of the dance floor and appeared to scan the crowd for a familiar face. His shaggy blond hair shone in the multicolored lights, and long lashes framed pale blue eyes. He was in a sleek black leather jacket and dark jeans. As I watched, he ran his fingers through that hair, sending shivers down my spine.

"Are you going to stand there like a statue all night, Celeste, or come show us your moves?" A voice beside me shook me out of my guy-ogling reverie.

"Emma, you're here!" I said a little too loudly. "Just hydrating before dancing," I covered, raising my cup to my lips and hoping she hadn't seen my eyes glued to the hottie.

"Well, finish that and come on! We need you in our girl circle of power," Emma said, her long light brown hair pulled into a sleek braid down her back, with curled tendrils framing her heart-shaped face.

Nodding, I drained my cup and turned to put it on the table behind her, surreptitiously taking another peek toward the entrance. A steady stream of people now flowed in through the door, but the new guy was nowhere to be seen.

I let my friends drag me out to the dance floor and tried to put the guy out of my mind. I hadn't found one yet who had held my interest past the first conversation. No doubt this one would be the same. I reminded myself to live in the moment and enjoy the night out, and to stop searching the crowd for a leather jacket.

~

"Dad, I'm home," I called as I walked in the door. I lived with my father in a modest two-bedroom house on Third Street, a short walk from both the high school and Miller's Plaza, where my dad's office was. He was a business accountant, keeping the books and doing taxes for several of the small businesses around town.

"You're home early," Dad replied, coming out of his study, where he spent most of his evenings during tax season. "How was the dance?"

"Oh, fine, just the same kids I see at school every day all dressed up," I said, hanging my coat by the door. Looking up to see my father's eyebrows pinched together, I quickly readjusted my own expression into a believable smile. "Fun. It was fun."

His face relaxed into a mirror of my own, and he gave a quick nod. "Good, well, there's lasagna in the fridge if you're hungry. I've got some more forms to finish up," he said, heading back toward his desk.

I went to my own room, getting ready for bed while I pondered a set of blue eyes framed by long lashes.

~

Even though I absolutely intended to sleep in on Friday, since we had a four-day weekend for Presidents' Day, I was up as usual at six in the morning. Unable to fall back to sleep, I got ready for my day. Emma, Gianna, and I had plans to go skiing later, but I had a few hours to kill, so I left a note for my dad, whom I could hear in the shower, and walked toward the town square. The sun was out, and the mountain air was fresh and mild. It would be a great day to hit the slopes.

I walked into Broastful Brew and ordered a coffee and a muffin, then settled in at my favorite corner table. It was a busy weekday morning, but early enough that most of the high school kids were probably still in bed. The town square was decorated with an explosion of heart decorations in pink and red. A beautiful woman with long black hair strode through the park in heels, still dressed in her slinky gown from the night before. I liked the peaceful, quiet vibe in the coffeehouse. I occasionally went to the other coffee shop in the square, Coffee Haven, if I happened to be shopping nearby, but I could have sworn I caught Willow giving me strange sideways looks whenever I went in there. It gave me the creeps. Mabel, the owner of Broastful Brew, always had a smile and a kind word for everyone.

As I gazed out at the square, I tuned out the conversations around me, until Irene Beckett's voice sounded from the table just behind me. She was a little old lady who used to teach at the high school decades ago and still thought she had the right to tell everyone how to live.

"Is that Tasha Young doing the walk of shame this morning?"

I glanced over to see her breakfast companion, Sybil Carson, who was always an eager audience for Mrs. Beckett's gossip. Usually they hung out at Coffee Haven, but I guessed they were here gathering information on someone or another.

"It looks more like a walk of pride to me," Sybil replied with a smile.

"Well, it's too bad she was never my student," Irene said, "or I'd have talked some decency into her. Look at that dress! It's fit for a—"

"Can I get you ladies anything else?" Mabel broke into their conversation just as Mrs. Beckett was about to lose her composure. I hid a giggle behind another bite of my muffin.

"No, thank you, dear," Mrs. Beckett said with an edge in her voice. "Have you seen the new woman in town yet? She's got a teenage son—it's just the two of them—and they just arrived this week."

"No," Mabel sighed, "they haven't been in here. I heard they're staying with Mrs. Walsh, so they probably go over to Coffee Haven for their caffeine."

"Well, don't you worry about that," Mrs. Beckett said. "One bite of those cookies, and they'll be hooked!"

"Why, thank you, Irene. Now I'd better get back to the counter. Let me know if you need anything!"

I focused back on my coffee. A new family in town, just this week. Could it be the guy I had spotted at the dance last night? I had kept an eye out for him the rest of the evening, but hadn't seen him again. I was beginning to think he was just an illusion.

Shrugging off the thought, I cleared my dishes to the counter and waved goodbye to Mabel. If he was at the dance, he'd be at school, and I'd find out soon enough who he was. But I had more important things to worry about. Like getting my ski on.

Purchase *Willful* where books are sold.